NICHOLAS CHANDLER

Off Season

WOLPH ENIX PUBLICATIONS

First edition

Cover photograph by the author

Published by Wolph Enix Publications
Edited by Ignatius Lamont

CHAPTER ONE

The warm rain fell sideways, hitting Marissa's face like gentle needles as she stood on the upper deck of the *Champion Jet 3*. Bundled in a denim jacket and struggling to keep her cigarette dry, she was exactly where she wanted to be. The engine's roar masked the soundings of the ocean birds that followed the wake. The ferry was pushing further away from Piraeus into the choppy expanse of the Aegean. She leaned against the gunwale railing to gaze at the southern horizon. The ocean spray dampened the soothing pain of the raindrops while the gust whipped her hair and smoked what remained of her wet cigarette. She could see the faint brown peaks of distant islands waiting for her through the light mist.

She had decided to stand outside for the duration of the three hour journey to Milos, having explained earlier to her boyfriend that even a minute inside would make her seasick. He was asleep in his seat the moment the engine started, his head resting on the backpacks stacked in the seat next to him. Marissa tossed what remained of her wet cigarette into the receptacle by the door and struggled against the wind to light another. Smoking in the rain didn't bother her in the slightest. It was just a part of the ecstasy of travel. It was her first time visiting Greece and the last few evenings in Athens had been more joyous than she had imagined. On their first night there, the couple had gotten drunk off cheap red wine, eaten souvlaki and mastic ice cream, then returned to their hotel for clumsy sex in front of a full sized mirror. Their shared apartment in Alphabet City didn't have a wall mirror by the bed so the inebriation combined with the act of watching herself have sex with her boyfriend was an almost out-of-body sensation, a rare treat. Aside from a quick obligatory visit to the Parthenon, the Erechtheion and Socrates' Prison, their first full day there was spent in much the same way - wandering the ancient streets and taking pictures while lazily searching for authentic meals between constant café stops to refuel on freddo espresso, spanakopita and cheap Marlboro Golds. The second night passed the same as the first - getting drunk on the same red wine and enjoying her own green eyes and bouncing breasts in the mirror, watching them fondled drunkenly by her boyfriend's vascular hands as he also watched, transfixed by the vision of his own lovemaking.

The door to the cabin beside her opened and a young woman stepped out huddled for warmth under a burgundy cowl, wearing dark Ray-Bans and an expensive looking leather jacket. She quickly moved under the feeble cover of the deckhouse roof that jutted out over the communal ashtray and stood shivering next to Marissa.

"Mind if I borrow a light?" she asked.

"Oh. Sure," Marissa replied, fishing a navy blue Bic from her breast pocket.

The woman pulled a pack of Marlboro Touch Blues from her purse and struggled to light one. During the twenty second battle against the wind, Marissa noticed the health warnings on the side of the box were Turkish.

"Thanks," the woman said, handing back the lighter after

2

defeating the wind. The first puff of the cigarette stopped her shivering.

"No problem. You get those in Türkiye?"

"Yeah. I just spent the last month there. Just explored a bit."

"Oh nice. I've always wanted to go there."

"Yeah, Yeah, It was a good time. A bit of a bore though," she said with a thick Australian accent.

"Really? From what I've seen online it looks incredible there."

"Can be hard to find alcohol on a budget's the issue. It's a bit more accommodating here."

"I could see that. I really like your jacket," said Marissa, tapping out her cigarette on the grates of the receptacle and grabbing another.

"Thank you. Thrifted. Found it in Paris a few months back."

"That's a great find."

"I know, right? I'm Cherry by the way. What brings you to the islands?"

"Marissa," she said, moving her hand slightly towards her chest. "I'm here for two weeks with my boyfriend, Zack. He's asleep inside. We're going to Milos, then Folegandros, then some other island he wanted to see before going to Santorini."

"Folegandros is supposed to be beautiful. I'm heading there myself to meet up with a group of friends for a few days."

A strong gust of wind drove in off the port side, kissing Marissa's face with sea spray and half blowing off Cherry's cowl, revealing previously well tucked balayage highlights. Cherry's lips were dark red, matching her name, and under her faux blonde hair were cherry pair earrings, similar to a slot machine's depiction. Marissa noticed her maroon manicured nails as she readjusted her windstrewn effects and removed her sunglasses to wipe the salty water off the lenses with the edge of her tank top. Marissa hadn't realised that what was left of her cigarette was completely saturated. She was fixedly noticing Cherry's irises - an almost mesmerizing tigerseye, especially as the sun's rays pierced them momentarily. Cherry put her glasses back on and smiled at Marissa.

"Thanks again for the light. Nice to meet you," she said.

"Yeah. No problem. Nice to meet you too," her words came out flustered. "I'll be out here if you need another."

"You're just going to stand outside the whole way?"

"I get seasick."

"I've got some sleeping pills if you want one."

"That's okay. Thanks. It's not so much the seasickness. I just like being outside on the ocean. I could watch the water for hours - even if we were in a hurricane. Actually, I'd probably enjoy that more. It's relaxing to watch a stormy sea and if I were sitting inside it just wouldn't feel the same."

"Whatever floats your boat. See you around," said Cherry before pushing the heavy iron door open and staggering, as gracefully as one can on a medium sized ferry pushing through choppy water, back to her seat.

The mainland disappeared over the northern horizon and Marissa had passed the last two hours by pacing around the deck and lighting a new cigarette every fifteen minutes with the occasional break to sit on a wet bench and scroll through her phone. She looked up restaurants and beaches on Milos and confirmed the address of the seaside cottage where they would be staying. But as the boat moved away from the storm and she smoked, staring at the islands in the distance - their light brown lifelessness contrasting the dark blue sea - she couldn't help but think about the girl she'd met whose name matched her earrings.

CHAPTER TWO

"Hey! You've been outside this whole time? We should try to be the first ones off the boat so we can get to the car rental place before everyone else," said Zack, energized from his nap. Marissa had just entered the cabin for the first time since depositing her backpack on her seat.

"We still have a few minutes. I don't think it'll be an issue."

Zack threw his backpack on his shoulder and checked his watch.

"We have four minutes," he said.

"That's enough time to grab a coffee."

"Not really. We can hit a café by the port. If we don't get a car, we're fucked. The Airbnb's on the other side of the island."

October was the off-season in the islands and there was a strong dry wind blowing from the south. As forceful as it was, it did nothing to stop the ferry from skillfully maneuvering astern into port. Zack and Marissa stood behind the chains of the gangway, watching as the Greek dockhand secured the line with practiced haste and fluidity. Once the ferryman raised the chain and gave the go-ahead, the young couple crossed the gangway, immediately feeling the force of the wind against them. While Zack beelined to the car rental agency beside the port, Marissa waited for him at the café next door. She thanked the waiter after he brought her a Greek coffee, then lit a cigarette and watched the other passengers disembark and slowly diffuse onto the island like a muddy river meeting the sea. Without judgment, she noticed the visual distinction between the locals and the other American tourists. The clothes, the hats, the clumsy movements and awestruck faces - all so distinguishable. She wondered if she looked like them. To a local? Certainly.

Her coffee was thick with sediment, but tasted rich and deep. As she drank it slowly, she saw Zack following a tall uniformed man with long hair, tied back in a ponytail. They were on their way to inspect the car. Why didn't he take a moment just to appreciate this place?, she thought. In the heavy wind, the whitecaps in the harbor reflected sunlight like diamonds. The Greek flags on the small docked boats fluttered violently, clinging onto their staves, and with each periodic mellow in the gust, let gravity calm them before starting their dance again. The smell of the harbor was unusually pleasant - a mixture of salty air and diesel swept away by a crisp early-autumn breeze.

Marissa looked up and saw Zack waving to grab her attention. He beckoned for her to come. She finished her coffee and put out her cigarette, left a few euros on the table and walked over to him.

"Well? What do you think?" he smiled. Beside him stood a baby blue Jeep Wrangler.

"Cute," she said, smiling back at him.

"We got pretty lucky. It was all they had left. I had to pay a little more but it's not a big deal."

"So we're ready to go now?"

"Yeah, let's do it!"

In the driver's seat of the Jeep, Zack entered the address of the Airbnb into the GPS and saw that it would take twenty five minutes to get across the island. The engine had already been turned on by the car rental employee so Zack put the car in drive and moved slowly through the small town of Adamantas, getting a feel for what was one of the largest cars on the island.

"Does this thing have bluetooth?" asked Marissa.

"Yeah. Why?"

"I wanna play some music."

"I think I have to pull over and turn off the car to pair a new device."

"Could you?"

"We've only got fifteen more minutes before we get there. Couldn't we just do it later?"

"We're not in a hurry, are we?"

"Well, no but..."

"Would you rather just drive there in silence? I mean, that's fine too I guess."

"Fine. I'll pull over," he resigned, turning off the empty road onto the dirt beside it.

Zack clicked the start button and the engine turned off. He stepped out of the Jeep and grabbed a Newport from the pocket of his jeans. He lit it and walked around the car to look at the sea while Marissa connected her phone to the system. It was the middle of the afternoon and the wind had died down a bit. He was scrolling through Instagram and smoking his menthol cigarette when Marissa told him she'd connected her phone.

"Come join me for a second. It's actually pretty nice here," he said, smiling peacefully as he turned to her.

She stepped down from the passenger side and stood next to him in the dirt beside the sea. The coastal road was lined with olive trees whose leaves rustled in what remained of the wind. She took a Marlboro Gold from her breast pocket and he lit it for her. Their first peaceful moment on the islands. Marissa looked upward at her boyfriend and felt secure and tranquil. He'd arranged every logistical component of their vacation. She loved his capable hands, his fashionable lack of fashion, his light blue eyes, his curled brown hair, his chevron moustache... He was wearing a red flannel shirt, a pair of washed blue Levi's and army green Mizunos. Under his sleeve was an Omega Seamaster his father had given him when he graduated college and started working at his uncle's investment banking firm. She didn't ask him much about his work and he rarely came home feeling stressed by it.

Marissa had graduated from San Diego State University before moving to New York to share an apartment with some of her high school friends. She had worked various jobs - bartender, saleswoman in a boutique clothing store, assistant at a marketing agency - but found a niche in the last year as a professional dog walker. She had a solid clientele and was earning enough money every month to pay her half of the rent and still save considerably.

They finished their cigarettes, snuffed them out in the dirt and climbed back into the Jeep.

"I think something's wrong," said Zack as he looked around the steering wheel inquisitively.

"Hmm?"

"I can't get the car to start."

"Didn't you start it earlier?"

"No, the guy started it for me. Fuck."

"Relax. I'm sure it's fine. We're not stuck here," Marissa placed her hand on Zack's shoulder.

"This fucking thing. I push the button to start and the engine doesn't do shit."

"Is your foot on the brake?"

"Yes," he said, his frustration growing.

"Maybe it has to be in a certain gear?"

"It's in park."

"Want to call the guy who started it earlier?"

"No. I'll figure it out."

He kept pressing the start/stop button to no avail.

"Fuck!" he shouted.

"Let me try," Marissa said calmly.

"Sure. Go ahead. If you think you can do it."

She stepped down and walked around to the driver's side. Zach got out and gestured for her to have a seat, mocking a *voiturier*. She checked the handbrake and saw the car was in park. She put her foot firmly on the brake pedal and pressed the start/stop button one time. The engine roared into life.

"What the fuck?" said Zack, astonished but relieved.

"I don't know. I just pressed hard on the brake while pressing the button. Maybe you weren't pushing hard enough?"

"I guess so," he said as she stepped down and returned to her side.

They continued along the coastal road until turning towards the center of the island. The roads were narrow and the hills around them were rocky and tan. The scenery reminded Marissa of trips to Baja she'd taken with her family when she was a kid.

10

"Well since I started the car, I get to be the DJ," she said jokingly.

"Go for it."

Her first choice was *Someday* by The Strokes. They snaked over another narrow hillside road and the modern world fell away from them. Nothing about their surroundings seemed to have changed in the last sixty years. Old dilapidated wooden fences lining dusty fields, the occasional olive tree, a small herd of domestic goats desperately rooting out any foliage in the aridity... Her second song choice was *Dance Hall* by Mrs. Green Apple. As the song crescendoed, the ocean came back into view from the windshield as they topped a hill and they saw the little house by the sea where they would be staying for the next two nights. Marissa giggled in excitement. Zack smiled too.

Five minutes later, they pulled into the driveway beside the cottage. There was an orange cat napping on a chair and out of the back door stepped an old Greek woman wearing a long cream colored dress patterned in yellow flowers. Her back was hunched, her skin had leathered under the Aegean sun and her hair was light grey.

"Hello. I'm Zack. Is this the Airbnb?" he smiled at the old lady.

She replied in Greek.

"Do you speak English?" he said.

"No English," she said slowly.

Marissa smiled at her before stepping around the car and grabbing their backpacks from the backseat. The old lady motioned for them to follow her and she showed them to the small apartment attached to the cottage. Beneath a covered patio overlooking the sea was the unlocked door to their lodgement. The room was quaint but perfect. Muted by cloud cover, dim sunlight shone through the southward facing window, gently illuminating a queen sized bed. At the other side of the room was a kitchenette equipped with coffee, milk, olive oil and a small loaf of rusk. Zack thanked the lady and she smiled at them. Marissa smiled excitedly and chirped "Efcharistó" to which the old lady replied "Parakalo" before walking back to her side of the cottage.

"She seems nice!" Marissa said, tossing her backpack on the bed.

"I bet she makes the best food. I'd kill to be invited to her table," Zack said, looking through the kitchen cabinets.

"Yeah. Probably best not to ask though."

"Yeah... I guess that would be rude," He put his hands on his hips, subtly indicating his want to leave the room. "Well, what should we do now? Should we go to the beach?"

"Hmmm. We should probably make sure the bed works first," said Marissa.

It only took a few minutes for the room to become messy with their clothes littering the floor and their backpacks tossed by the sides of the bed. In those same minutes, the wind outside picked up again and blew with such a force that it whistled as it wove through the dried bamboo side paneling on the patio. The wind was forecasted to cool and continue for the next two days, bringing with it a relentless rainfall.

CHAPTER THREE

Taylor Swift's *The Fate of Ophelia* played through the Jeep's speakers as the couple zigzagged through the island's winding roads. The man at the car rental desk had advised them that due to the heavy wind, the northern beaches would be more calm and ideal for swimming. To cross the island in any direction took about half an hour, so it wasn't long before they arrived at a small cove with white sand and clear water. Zack held the beach bag as Marissa followed him from the parking lot and over a small rocky outcrop to a secluded enclave, separate from the main beach. Sheltered from the south wind, the deposit of soft warm sand no larger in area than a California king sized mattress was the ideal place for them to set down their beach towels. Once they'd stripped to their swimwear and taken repose, Marissa grabbed an unopened book from the tan linen tote - *A Wild Sheep Chase* by Haruki Murakami. Zack leaped up from his towel and asked Marissa if she was good. After she smiled and nodded at him, he ran into the water, splashing energetically like a labrador retriever.

The sun peeked out through the quickly rolling clouds, beaming strong light into the water and clarifying it for a few minutes before returning to hiding. Zack felt the relief of the sunshine on his back as he swam deep into the cool October water. Each time the sunshine faded, the water would darken and he was unable to see his own legs under the depths. Every so often, he'd stop to tread water, look at the droplets on his Seamaster and gaze back at Marissa, reclining on her towel with her head propped up to read. She was wearing a brown bikini and sunglasses and her medium length brown hair fell just past her shoulders. *I'm a lucky man*, he thought. *An empty beach in the Greek Islands, a beautiful girlfriend - this is my life for the next two weeks. I wish I could stay here forever.*

The character in the Murakami book was talking about his alcoholism and his indifference to his recent divorce. The depression imbued in the text was almost alluring as Marissa flipped through the pages, engrossed in the narrative. After half an hour of reading, she'd cleared a few chapters. The main character had met a young woman with perfect ears, and Marissa found herself struggling to pay attention. Her thoughts drifted to the woman with the deep red lipstick and the earrings that matched her name. Cherry. *It would be nice to have a friend here*, she thought. She placed her bookmark into the page and set the novel on the towel beside her before untying her bikini top, rolling onto her back and closing her eyes. An hour under the sun without wind was absolute bliss after the stinging rain on the boat and the continuous gust that followed.

She was almost asleep when Zack ran out of the water.

"Wawaweewa. Very nice. How Much?" he said, affecting Borat's accent.

Marissa lazily turned to her side to face him.

"How's the water?"

"So good," he said, taking an upright seat on the beach towel opposite hers.

"Really? Not too cold?"

14

"Yeah. It's not bad. Feels good in the sun."

"Let me get a quick tan, then I'll join you for a swim?"

"Sounds good Babe."

As Marissa flipped back onto her stomach, resting her head on her arms, Zack scrolled through his phone and occasionally got up to take pictures of the small cove. He busily posted them to his Instagram story so his friends and associates back in New York could see the pristine Aegean beach as they rode the morning bus into Manhattan to settle into their offices. He grabbed his vacation book from the bag - Fleming's *Diamonds are Forever*. Two chapters into it, Marissa had woken up. She stood and stretched.

"Come swim with me," she said, her bare breasts drawing his attention.

"Let's go!" he replied, launching himself from his towel and running back into the sea.

"Oh my God! It's freezing!" Marissa screeched, ankle deep in the surf.

"Don't be a baby. Come on," he said before submerging his head in the water. He whipped his hair back and splashed some water at her. With her arms across her chest, she shivered as she slowly waded in. Once she had acclimated, she felt like it was actually reasonably warm but it wasn't long after they started swimming that the wind picked up again and even the northern side of the island became a little more than breezy. The gust carried with it an overwhelming chill and the surface water was starting to roughen. The couple returned to the sand and towelled themselves dry.

"Hey, Babe. Should we have sex?" asked Zack.

"Right here?!" Marissa chuckled. "It's so cold!"

"I can warm you up."

"Maybe later. It's way too cold. And what if somebody came?"

"Nobody's going to see. Come on..."

"Later."

"Fine. I love you."

"Love you too," she said, tying on her bikini top and putting back on her linen shirt and pants.

"Well, what should we do now?" asked Zack as he put on his J-Crew sweater and Knicks cap.

"I'd love a glass of wine."

"Let's do it."

As they were walking back over the rocks to the parking lot by the main stretch of beach, another couple passed them in the direction of their private enclave. Marissa glanced at Zack's eyes and smiled cheekily, as if to suggest *I told you so*.

Back in the Jeep, Marissa continued playing the new Taylor Swift album and Zack suggested ten minutes of silence.

"You're allergic to fun," she joked, pausing the music.

"I'm not *allergic to fun*. I just don't think this matches the vibe. I liked what you were playing earlier."

"But this album just came out today and I really want to listen to it."

"Young Thug just dropped an album today too but I'm not pushing it on you. I know you're not into it so I'll just listen to it on my own later."

"Fine. Silence it is," she pouted.

"It's just a few more minutes. There are some restaurants back near the port. I'm sure we'll find something good there."

They parked in a public lot and walked for about five minutes before choosing an outdoor table just next to the lapping water. After a brief struggle against the wind to light their cigarettes, a waitress came by their table and they ordered a bottle of local rosé. Zack took a picture of the bottle as it arrived at their table. The wine was chilled and delicious and the couple lit a new cigarette with each glass. Zack was a silent drinker and the small squabble in the car about music had soured the afternoon a bit. Except for the occasional "This is nice", they scrolled through their phones and drank hurriedly as the sun descended and the wind strengthened, heralding the coming night. Far on the horizon was a dark curtain of rainfall dampening the lustre of their first island sunset.

"I just made a reservation for the restaurant next to our Airbnb," said Zack, setting his phone face down on the table.

"When? I'm starving," Marissa put out her cigarette.

"Have you eaten today?"

"Not since we had those cheese pies in Athens."

"Me neither. I thought you may have grabbed something on the ferry. Dinner's in an hour and a half."

"Do you think they'd seat us if we were early?"

"This whole island seems pretty empty. I'm sure it won't be a problem. Should we head out?"

"Yeah. Let's just go home first so I can change."

CHAPTER FOUR

They drove back to the cottage in fatigued silence. As soon as they returned, Zack stripped naked, threw his damp swimsuit and sweater on the floor, and stepped into the shower. *That's going to reek*, thought Marissa, heaving a sigh. Before getting comfortable, she picked up his wet garments and hung them on the line outside on the patio. The blast of cold wind made her shiver. She took off her clothes and hung them on the same line then walked back inside naked and freezing.

"Make some room. I'm dying," she said, joining Zack in the shower. It was cramped and uncomfortable but the steam immediately soothed her.

"Mmmm," said Zack, looking down at the soap on his girlfriend's breasts. He grabbed her hips and rubbed his body against hers.

"What are you doing?" she asked, annoyed and trying to rinse off the seawater.

"Just enjoying my beautiful girlfriend," he said, grinning.

"Well you can enjoy her later."

"Alright. Shower's yours," he said before stepping out and toweling dry his hair.

Marissa was thankful to have the shower to herself and she closed

18

her eyes under the hot water until the steam blanketed the small room. When she was done, she wrapped herself in a bathrobe and applied moisturizer and makeup. When she left the restroom, she found Zack sitting outside on the patio. She stood in the doorway and noticed he was smoking a joint he had bought in Athens.

"Without me!?" she said jokingly.

"It's not even that good anyway."

"Still. Would have been fun to smoke it together."

"Don't worry. I still have a few more. I'm ready to go when you are. The restaurant's just down the hill. We could probably just walk there."

"Okay. I'll just be a few minutes."

Fifteen minutes later, Marissa had chosen a cute warm outfit for dinner - a long white skirt with a navy blue cardigan over a gray wool tank top. They still had thirty minutes before their reservation so they sat on the patio and each smoked a cigarette. While they discussed what they were going to order for their first dinner in the islands, the roar of the angry sea below the cliff and the whistle of the wind in the bamboo paneling hummed, as if nature was also hungry and jealous of their plans.

They walked down the dirt road and arrived at the restaurant where they were seated immediately in the center of the small room. Other couples were already seated at the tables next to the open walls beside the beach. Each minute after the sunset, the color of the sky changed from cerulean to black, one shade at a time.

"Would have been nice to get a window table," said Zack, putting down the menu.

"It's fine. I'm happy here."

"Still though. Would have made for a better picture."

"Can't you just enjoy an evening without thinking about the optics? Like, God. It would be so nice to just live in the moment and not make everything about Instagram. I don't get why you feel the need to share every part of your day with the whole world?"

"Sorry for enjoying myself. I'm just happy to be here with you and I like cataloging my experiences. It's not like I post shit so people can see it. I just do it for myself. It's fun."

"That doesn't make any sense."

"It doesn't have to. It does to me."

The lights of the beachfront lampposts switched on outside, shining a soft yellow glow on a beached wooden rowboat.

"It's not like I need to post. I won't take a picture of our dinner tonight. I'll *live in the moment*," said Zack, placing his phone on the edge of the table.

"I'm sorry I brought it up. I don't know what's wrong with me today. Maybe I'm just hungry."

"You look beautiful tonight,"

Marissa laughed.

"You're so full of shit," she said, smiling.

"I love you," he doubled down.

"I love you too."

They ordered a bottle of local white wine, oven roasted aubergine with olive oil and feta, grilled octopus over a bed of red pepper purée, and an entire red snapper. As soon as the first dish arrived, Zack looked at Marissa with puppy dog eyes.

"Fine. Take a picture. I know you want to," she said, just happy to have something to eat.

"I'll be quick."

The twenty five seconds of photography felt like an eternity as the *entrée* tempted her. Once Zack declared that he was done taking the picture, she helped herself to half of the eggplant. It was, undoubtedly, the best eggplant she'd ever tasted. The octopus was served to the center of their small table not long after and as they were cutting into it and serving themselves, rain started pouring into the restaurant through the open walls. Almost every other couple next to them stood up abruptly to escape the torrent. One woman stood so fast that she knocked over her chair before running into the dry part of the restaurant by the bar while the man accompanying her continued to sit and sip his red wine, indifferent to the lashing storm or his partner's discomfort. The waiters all rushed to secure plastic curtains over the walls and a few minutes later, the restaurant was insulated from the downpour. Half of the couples who had been sitting at the window tables lined up to pay their bill at the bar and left immediately and the other half laughed the whole thing off, ordered more wine and wiped their seats with their napkins while they waited for lobster or dessert.

"I guess we got pretty lucky," said Zack.

"It's not such a bad table after all, huh?"

The whole red snapper was brought tableside and the waiter masterfully deboned it, plucking out each transparent bone with tweezers before serving two plates worth of meat with a drizzle of lemon sauce.

"You know? I don't see how life can get any better than this," said Zack, sliding a bite of fish onto his fork.

"It's so fresh," Marissa remarked at the fish.

21

"No, well yeah, but no. I mean everything. Just being here with you, driving the Jeep, the rustic vibe... We should buy a vacation home here."

"That's a little ambitious, no?" Marissa said, taking another bite of snapper.

"I guess. But maybe we could retire in a place like this. You could be like that old woman and we could have goats and make feta."

"You want me to make cheese?"

"Why not? My aunt's husband, Wes - he retired a year ago and bought a dairy farm in Vermont. They split their time between there and their place in Boston. I could imagine something like that for us."

"Maybe. I mean, a pied-à-terre in Paris would be nice too."

"Fuck Paris. What's there to do there? It's just shopping and buttery food."

"*Fuck Paris*? Are you for real? It's the most romantic city in the world. And the food there isn't buttery."

"That's a city for women."

"Huh. Well you know what's crazy? It just so happens that I'm a woman. A reality that you enjoy very much when it's convenient for you."

"All I was saying is that it would be nice to live a simple life in the islands when we're old together."

"I know what you're saying but I'm telling you that maybe we could split time between here and somewhere else like a big city. And how can you not like Paris?"

"Why Paris? Why not Amsterdam or London or, hell, even New York?"

The waiter came to the table and refilled their wine glasses then set the bottle back in the ice bucket.

"Because. I've only been there once when I was twenty and I'd love to go back. I had a really good time there."

"When I went there with my family as a kid, I thought it was boring and other than french fries, all the food was bland."

"Well let's go together so we can make new memories."

"I guess. Maybe next year," he said, shutting down the conversation and finishing the fish on his plate.

The snapper had been caught the day before by an old fisherman who lived in Adamantas. He was inside his house eating avgolemono prepared by his wife of forty years. Both of his two adult sons were studying medicine in Athens. He'd sold the fish to the restaurant for seventeen euros after anchoring his boat for the coming storm. The restaurant was selling it for eighty five.

Once they'd finished the main course, the waiter came to clear their dishes and take their dessert order. Two pieces of galaktoboureko and two vieux carrés. Marissa was already a little tipsy from the continuous drip of wine since the afternoon but Zack felt like impressing her by taking the liberty of ordering a cocktail with a French name. She noticed a maraschino cherry at the bottom of the glass when the drink arrived.

It was still raining when they left the restaurant and they walked back to the cottage up the muddy hill in almost total darkness. Zack stepped inside and called one of his friends while Marissa smoked three cigarettes on the patio, listening to the rain and watching what little moonlight there was reflecting off the vast sea below the cliff. When she finished smoking and came inside, he asked her for sex but she was cold and exhausted.

"Maybe tomorrow," she said, climbing into bed and grabbing her book from the nightstand.

"I'll hold you to it," he said before turning off the light.

CHAPTER FIVE

At the highest peak on the island, in the town of Plaka, stood a small white church - only accessible by foot. In the courtyard before the blue door was a bronze bell that overlooked the sea. Abandoned farm beds sat at the foot of the rocky peak and opposite them were the remnants of agricultural terraces resembling Incan andenes. *This was once an incredible place*, thought Marissa as she stopped to catch her breath on the steep narrow path coming down from the chapel. Zack was ahead of her, farther down the path. He had found the church boring and started his descent while Marissa was looking inside. Below the church, the Ancient Theater of Milos had been carved into the hillside thousands of years ago and beside it, next to the parking lot where the Jeep rested, stood a replica of the Venus de Milo - indicating the location of its discovery.

"It says here that the real one's in the Louvre," said Zack, reading the plaque on the statue while Marissa took pictures.

"Oh yeah. I remember seeing it a few years ago."

"That's the French for you... taking things that don't belong to them."

"I think I remember reading somewhere that the French actually paid for it."

"Like how the Dutch 'bought' Manhattan? It's always white

people taking advantage of everybody else."

"I'm not sure if you realize this Zack, but you're white."

"I'm just saying..."

He's probably just grumpy because I didn't fuck him this morning, thought Marissa. The ground was still wet from the overnight rain. The storm had passed in the early morning and the wind had subdued. Another squall was predicted for that evening, but they were going to catch the afternoon ferry and be on their way to the next island by then.

"You trying to eat something?" said Zack, eager to move on.

"Sure. Any ideas?"

"Yeah I saw a place earlier that looked nice. It's just back in town."

Marissa pulled a cigarette from the breast pocket of her denim jacket and lit it.

"Sounds good," she said.

Stopping to take a final look at the theater draped on the hill below her, she wondered what plays had been performed there. She imagined ancient islanders meandering the narrow footpaths down from the village and gathering to watch Euripides or Sophocles. On those stone seats, people cried while performers sang and a young actor playing Hippolytus, chaste and dying, forgave his father for his unjust exile. *They would have been drinking the same wine and eating the same cheeses and feeling the same emotions as I do when I watch Netflix*, she thought.

"You coming?" Zack called out, already half way back to the car.

Marissa took a long last drag from her cigarette, put it out on the bottom of her shoe, and held onto the butt so as to litter in the parking lot and not the ancient hillside.

It didn't take longer than five minutes to drive up the hill and park the Jeep in a communal dirt lot in Plaka. From there, the couple walked along an empty road to a tavern with a courtyard shaded by olive trees. A few cats were curled up, resting on chairs and waiting to beg for food when the time came. Behind a counter in the courtyard stood an older Greek man, bald with tan skin and a thick white moustache. He was smoking a cigarillo while marinating pork. Zack stepped inside to ask the hostess for an outdoor table. Because it had just opened for the day, they were the only guests at the tavern. Once they'd selected their table and seated themselves, a middle aged woman with black hair took a break from folding dolmades to present them with menus and take their drink order. Zack asked for two glasses of white wine and they glanced at the menu briefly before deciding and each lighting a cigarette.

"So what time is the ferry?" asked Marissa.

"It leaves a little after five. I figured after this, we could head back to the Airbnb to pack up then head down to the port."

"Cool," she said. Tendrils of blue smoke wafted upward from the tip of her Marlboro as she turned her attention to one of the sleeping cats. It yawned and stretched then got up to walk around.

"So I was talking to Noah last night..."

"Yeah? How is he?" Marissa interjected, her mind returning to the table.

"He's fine, I guess. But not really. He thinks he's going to break up with Safa."

"Really? Why? She's so cool."

"I know. He's such an idiot. He told me he doesn't like that she

27

posts about Palestine all the time."

"He can't be serious," Marissa said, suppressing a shocked laugh.

"Yeah. I tried telling him he's dumb as fuck and that he probably shouldn't have dated a Kuwaiti woman if he felt so strongly about Israel."

"She's too good for him anyway."

"Well, he's a great guy. Don't get me wrong. He's just objectively wrong about this one issue and it just sucks that politics can end a relationship. Like, I told him his opinion is just straight up incorrect."

"Did he get mad?" Marissa lit another cigarette.

"No. We respect each other. We've known each other since the playground. But I told him that Israel used to be Bedouin before Abraham, and even then, he migrated into what they call *the Promised Land* and so by their own definition they aren't even indigenous to that land. Then he said neither are the Palestinians, and like, I agreed with him and told him about how the Pharaoh conquered Israel and the Philistines sailed in from Anatolia shortly after,"

"But saying that you're entitled to land because you're ancestors are from there doesn't justify killing babies,"

"Exactly. That's how the conversation ended. It doesn't matter who owned the land thousands of years ago. I mean, private property as a concept didn't even exist back then. It was just a bunch of tribes settling on common land and fighting over water rights. In the end, he agreed that killing babies is wrong and I told him not to let some bullshit in the middle east affect his sex life. It's self sabotage."

"Why does he feel so strongly about it? He doesn't go to temple. I've seen him eat pork."

"God knows..."

The black haired woman came to take their order - dolmades, a greek salad, stuffed zucchini in avgolemono, wood fired local lamb, and the rest of the bottle of the wine they were drinking.

"We're going to be ten pounds heavier by the time we get home," said Marissa.

"We could burn some calories later if you're interested."

"Is that why you ordered the bottle?"

"Of course not. It's just good. I think it's from Santorini. You excited to be there soon?"

"Yeah. It looks incredible."

The dolma and salad were brought out almost instantly with the rest of the opened bottle and they were eaten within minutes. A small orange cat had made itself cozy under their table and Marissa reached down to stroke its head. It knew the restaurant's pattern and probably smelled the lamb cooking before the couple could. The man marinating pork at the outdoor counter wiped his forehead with a towel, put out his cigarillo and went inside to make himself a coffee. After a few silent moments of scrolling through Instagram, the zucchini and lamb arrived at the table simultaneously with a basket of bread. The meat was tender and fell off the bone. It tasted sweet, mildly seasoned with lemon and herbs.

"So, how many more months until Rebecca has her baby?" asked Marissa.

"I guess like two or three," said Zack, focused on the meal.

"Are you going to visit her when your niece is born?"

"Fly to Boulder in late December? I'd rather not."

"You should. It's a big deal becoming an uncle. Your mom will be there."

"It sounds awful. Maybe if you come with me. But I don't know if I can take the time off work."

"We could just go for a weekend. It's family."

"Yeah. It's not like the baby will have any idea who I am. It won't remember shit," he said with a mouthful of zucchini.

"It's not about the baby. It's about your sister. And your mom."

"Ok, fine. I'll buy us tickets when we get home. I don't want to worry about it now."

"Is your dad going to go see his first grandson?"

"I don't think he's invited. Rebecca still isn't talking to him. If he really cared he wouldn't have run off to Saint Lucia or wherever he is with his new girlfriend. We all make our choices I guess."

"I hate to say it cuz it's your dad but it seems like he's still being an asshole."

"Yeah. He wasn't always. It is what it is. You going to eat the rest of that lamb?"

"Go for it," Marissa offered, wiping her lips with her napkin and putting it on her plate before fishing out another Marlboro.

"I wish we could just stay in the islands forever," said Zack, grabbing the meat with his hands and consuming every part of cartilage on the bone like Saturn devouring his son. Marissa had only finished two glasses of wine as Zack poured his fourth.

After lunch, they drove back to the cottage so they could get ready to leave Milos. Marissa insisted on taking the wheel since Zack had asked for a shot of ouzo after drinking most of the wine. The sky was cloudy and the hills beside them were golden brown as they listened to *Pop Out* by Playboi Carti on loop - Zack's drunken request. Once they returned to their apartment overlooking the sea, Marissa obliged the inevitable second drunken request. After taking a quick shower together and putting their clothes back on, they quickly stuffed their clothes in their backpacks and shared one of the Athenian joints on the patio.

They dropped the car off in Adamantas. While Zack handled the return, Marissa stopped at a small shop to buy more Marlboro Golds. She then joined him at the same café where she'd ordered Greek coffee the previous day. Today's order was a freddo cappuccino. It wasn't long before the small ferry docked at the port and they were ushered into the cabin. Once they'd boarded the *Super Jet 2*, Marissa took a lap around the boat and realized there was no outdoor access so she'd have to spend an hour in her seat. When the ferry got underway, the rocking of the waves and the acrid smell of the diesel exhaust made Marissa sick. She rushed out of her seat to vomit in the restroom. She felt a little relieved but not enough to return to her seat. She curled up on the floor in a pile of suitcases and backpacks and tried to close her eyes. After noticing she'd been gone a while, Zack got up to find her and upon seeing her sleeping like a restaurant cat, smiled, covered her with his flannel, and returned to his seat to watch anime on his phone.

CHAPTER SIX

The sun was beginning to set over a cloudless sky as they arrived at the port of Karavostasis and saw a uniformed man holding a sign, waiting for them. They were ushered into his Mercedes van and driven up the winding hillside road into the town of Chora. After being dropped off at a resort at the edge of the town, Zack went to the reception desk to check in while Marissa surveyed the property. The expansive two story building, washed white by the sun, wrapped around a large central pool bordered by palm trees, umbrellas, and reclining chairs. Still feeling the lingering effect of seasickness, she desperately wanted to settle in so she could shower and brush her teeth. They were shown to their room on the second floor - a cozy, traditional room with white walls and thick wooden beams on the roof. Beside the bed was a thick gray curtain drawn beside an open French door that led to a private patio with a small wooden table and a view of the neighboring white rooftops. The sea sparkled far in the distance.

Marissa wasted no time grabbing her toiletry kit from her backpack and rushing into the restroom to perform the ablutions required after seafaring. While she showered, Zack sat on the patio and enjoyed the last of the Athenian joints he'd purchased while watching the sky turn yellow. Up a zigzagging footpath at the top of the cliff beside the town was a monastery and as he puffed at his joint, he thought it would be a beautiful place to watch the sunset before taking Marissa to dinner. He suggested it to her while she dried her hair. She agreed.

The narrow flagstone paths that ran through the town were jointed with white lime and lined with rustic white-walled homes draped in fully bloomed bougainvilleas. As they walked through the ancient streets, they could smell the souvlaki roasting in the taverns. It didn't take long for them to reach the opposite edge of town and begin their ascent towards the island's most iconic vista point. The closer they got to the church, the smaller Chora became and the sea surrounding them grew visible from every angle. After reaching the monastery's courtyard, they sat on the short white wall that lined it and watched as the sky transformed into a variegated palette of crimson, violet, green and gold. Zack reached his arm around Marissa and pulled her gently towards him. She nestled her head on his shoulder, enjoying an almost mystical silence. Far away from the noise of the city, the world, in this instant, existed only for them. The stars illuminated the indigo heavens minutes after the sun touched the horizon and Marissa kissed Zack then lit a cigarette. They sat for a while longer, enjoying the deep celestial quiet above them before a chilled wind compelled them to stroll leisurely back down the zigzagging path.

"I know a really good place where we can grab dinner," Zack said in a calm voice, so as not to disturb the evening's serenity.

"I'm down for whatever," she responded, puffing her Marlboro.

"This place had great reviews. And I saw this picture on Yelp. There's this pasta that's the island's specialty. It's super old and they serve it with a dark red sauce. I forgot what it's called. Let me show you."

He took his phone from his pocket to look up the dish as Marissa tapped out her cigarette with her foot and lit another. As she stopped to do so, she looked up to notice more stars dancing each minute. How long had it been since she'd been in a place unpolluted by artificial light? She couldn't remember. And even back on Milos, the cloud cover had blocked the starlight.

"Matsata!" Zack declared, showing Marissa the name of the pasta on his phone. "I don't think I'll ever be able to remember that."

"Yeah. It doesn't really roll off the tongue. Looks good though."

"I know, right? And it's traditionally topped with rabbit or goat."

Back in the town, the streetlights had turned the house's façades buttermilk yellow and the aroma of stewed and grilled meat wafted through the alleyways. Tourists and locals both were seated outside at the few open watering holes and teenagers stood in circles in the central plaza, talking boisterously, gossiping and planning the evening. They approached the restaurant and saw a sign on the door that said, in both English and Greek, "Closed for the Season. See You Next Year!"

"Damn," said Zack. "This place looked good too."

"It's not a big deal. Everything smells great. Let's just go to that place next door."

"Yeah. Okay. I guess so," he sighed.

Marissa made eye contact with the smiling half bald waiter clearing a table outside a tavern.

"Two?" she asked.

"Anywhere you like," he said, smiling back warmly.

They sat next to an old couple with an almost empty bottle of wine at their table. Tiny lights hung on rope from the bougainvilleas that arched over the red gingham covered tables, mimicking the stars. The waiter brought two menus and a basket of bread. Three cats slept in a triangle on the stone floor next to their table. After they'd ordered pies with local goat cheese, a greek salad, and two plates of rabbit matsata accompanied by a carafe of red wine, a group of eight young people were seated at four small tables pushed together behind them. Marissa couldn't help but notice the familiar hair of the woman she'd met on the ferry two days earlier. This time, she wore earrings with sequined scarlet hearts and her dark golden eyes looked larger due to a strong application of eyeliner. She noticed Marissa and raised her hand in a casual wave. Marissa smiled back and raised her glass of water at her. Zack turned his head to see who she was looking at.

"You know that girl?" he asked.

"Yeah. I met her on the ferry to Milos. She asked me for a light."

"Oh. That's cool," he said, seemingly uninterested. "So I was thinking tomorrow we could rent an ATV and explore the island a bit. I found some beaches I want to check out. What do you think?"

"I said earlier. I'm down for whatever."

"Are you mad at me?" he asked.

The waiter came with the carafe of wine and poured them each a glass.

"No. What makes you say that?" Marissa replied after the brief interruption. She grabbed her glass and took a sip.

"I don't know. You seem a bit off. We haven't been talking much and you've been smoking a lot more than you do back home. I just thought you'd be more excited to be here with me."

"Of course I'm happy to be here with you. I'm not mad at you. Are you mad at me?"

"I love you. I could never be mad at you. I couldn't imagine being here if it wasn't with you. Remember that first night in Athens? The way the Parthenon was all lit up. The ambiance of the city... This whole trip so far has been absolutely incredible."

"Yeah. It has."

"You know? One day we're going to look back at this time in our lives, when we were young and we lived in a tiny apartment and all we really had was each other. We should cherish these moments. Here's to right now," Zack toasted, raising his glass. "And to whatever the future holds."

"Cheers!" Marissa clinked her glass against his and took another sip.

Cherry's group was laughing and getting loud before the alcohol even touched their table. From the conversation Marissa overheard, she could tell that each friend was from a different country. One had come from Mexico, one from Germany, one from England, etc... From the register of their voices, most of them seemed gay and that was confirmed as they continued their rapid-fire discourse, gossiping about who was still with who and what countries they'd visited in the last year.

While Zack and Marissa ate their salad and cheese pies, they both eavesdropped as one of the young men from Cherry's table told the old couple they were very cute as they started on their desserts.

"Thank you," the old woman replied. She had three gold bracelets on her wrist and was draped in a cream colored cape.

"How long have you been together?" asked the young man.

"Forty three years," she replied without a moment of hesitation.

"Oh my God. That's incredible. Congratulations. What's your secret? What advice could you give us?" he asked, either overly social or already inebriated. The rest of the table turned their attention to her answer. The old woman's reply was spoken softly. At the same moment, Zack was asking the waiter for another carafe of wine while their plates were being cleared so Marissa couldn't make out what she said.

"Wow. I'm going to remember that. Where are you from?" he asked the old couple, refusing to let them enjoy their yogurt and honey.

"We're from Denmark," replied the old man curtly.

"And is it your first time here?" the young man asked as the waiter moved to his table to take his friends' orders.

"No. We've been renting a house here for two months each year for the last twenty years," said the woman. She was happy to answer his line of questioning. "We like this island. It's very quiet during this season."

"That's so sweet. I'll let you enjoy your evening. So nice to meet you!" he said.

"You too. Enjoy your time here," the old woman replied. Her husband pulled out his wallet and put some cash on the table. They both got up and strolled away, leaving their wine unfinished.

Zack had just ordered two bowls of local yogurt with honey when the large group behind him was being served their plates of chicken souvlaki and fries. One of the men asked for ketchup. They were all drinking beers and shots of ouzo. Marissa lit another cigarette then noticed the cats had just awakened from their slumber and were starting to beg for souvlaki. Without saying a word, Zack stood up to go inside the restaurant. Now sitting alone, Marissa looked across the table at Cherry and they locked eyes for more than a few seconds. Cherry, in no hurry to eat her chicken, pulled a Marlboro Touch Blue from her pack on the table and lit it. She was the only woman in the group.

Zack returned grinning and holding a full bottle of ouzo and two shot glasses.

"Are you serious?" asked Marissa, laughing.

"Looks fun. Come on. Let's let loose tonight."

"I'm already pretty tipsy."

"Well, just have a little then. We wouldn't want you to get too fucked up. I'm pretty much sober," he lied, pouring two shots. He threw his back and poured another. Marissa took a small sip from hers. It had a strong bite under the anisette flavor. She didn't like it.

"I'm going to use the bathroom real quick," she said, resting her cigarette in the ashtray then sliding her chair back to stand up.

"'Kay Babe," said Zack, picking up his phone from the table.

Inside the tavern, a short old woman wearing a dirty apron was microwaving something while a bearded man who could have been her husband was roasting lamb and chicken. A frail looking elderly man sat in the corner, smoking a cigarillo and uninterestedly watching a football match. The waiter looked at Marissa and asked her if she was looking for a restroom. She nodded and he pointed to a door at the back of the tavern.

After standing up and flushing the toilet, she felt a rush of lightheadedness and grabbed the sink to support herself. *He's right. I've been smoking too much*, she thought. She lifted her head and looked in the mirror. Her teeth were starting to yellow. She still had the glow of youth though, and the clear whites of her eyes surrounded her green irises like the lime washed walls of the buildings outside, dappled with leaves. She delighted at her wavy brown hair in the reflection and reached into her purse to reapply her lipstick.

When she returned to the table, she noticed half the bottle of ouzo was gone and Zack was already devouring his bowl of yogurt. Hers was still waiting for her.

"Did you seriously just drink all that just now?" she asked, picking up her spoon.

"What?" he replied with his mouth full.

"Half the bottle's gone!"

Zack paused his ravenous eating and looked at the bottle.

"Huh. Somebody drank my ouzo! It was just here a minute ago."

"You're drunk," she said, still having not touched her dessert.

"I'm fine. Here, have another shot," he poured more liquor into Marissa's cup and it overflowed. "Oops. My bad. Maybe I'm a little drunk," he admitted, before pouring himself another and knocking it back in one smooth motion.

Marissa sighed and took a bite of the yogurt. She couldn't identify exactly why, but it was the best yogurt she'd ever tasted. She wanted to savor it. She decided to light another cigarette and enjoy the rest of her dessert in a few minutes.

"You don't want it?" Zack said, looking at her bowl with confused lustful eyes, like a thirteen year old boy who'd just found a pornographic magazine for the first time in his dad's closet.

"No. It's really good. I'm going to eat it slowly," she said, puffing at her cigarette.

"You sure you don't want it?" he said, sinking his spoon into her bowl to grab a bite right from the center where the honey was most concentrated.

"What the fuck Zack! I said I wanted it!"

"Oh. Sorry Babe. I heard 'No'. I thought you wanted me to have it."

"Just take it. I don't care."

"No. No. I'm sorry. I can order you another one."

"No. Just have it. I'm fine."

"If you insist..." he grabbed the bowl and devoured it like an animal, as though he'd just escaped from a prison camp during a war and hadn't eaten a proper meal in years. Then he poured himself another shot of ouzo.

When Zack staggered inside to pay the bill, Marissa put out her halfway smoked cigarette and drank the ouzo in her glass, wincing at the taste. She looked up again at Cherry. She was resting her head in her hands and listening to a story one of her friends was telling. The white smoke from the barely touched Marlboro tucked beside her chin floated whimsically to the pink flowers above her. She laughed at the story then daintily puffed her cigarette.

"We're all set," said Zack, walking out of the tavern. "I'm spinning a little bit."

"No shit. You had most of the wine and a full bottle of ouzo."

"We shared it. You're drunk too. We could get more if you're not."

"No. I'm drunk," she lied. She was feeling the effect of the alcohol, but not to the level of full inebriation. She got up from the table and supported him as he sauntered through the town, swerving as though his ankles were made of custard.

"Let's get you home," Marissa said softly, guiding him back to the resort.

"Let's s-stop for gelato," he was slurring his words.

"I think you need to rest."

"You hate fun," he said. "Fun Hater."

"Yeah, yeah. I hate fun. Let's get you to bed."

"My girlfriend hates fun. I'm fun. My girlfriend hates me. She won't let me have ge-la-to."

Marissa sighed.

Ten long minutes later, she led him up the stairs to the room where Zack immediately collapsed onto the bed like a felled tree. He muttered something indecipherable and started snoring.

CHAPTER SEVEN

An ethereal starlight flooded in through the open patio doors, accompanied by a faint October breeze. Dim yellow streetlamps blanketed the island village, shielding it from darkness like fireflies in a clearing surrounded by thick forest. At the outdoor table, Marissa sat lazily puffing the penultimate cigarette in her pack. The purifying night air blanketed her, inching her closer to sobriety with every passing minute. She could still hear music and laughter echoing weakly rising from the alleys. Moonlight fell onto the sea far below the hillside town and danced on the ripples of the surface.

Once she'd finished the pack, Marissa came back inside and closed the door behind her. She covered her diagonal and comatose boyfriend with the blanket at the foot of the bed then quietly grabbed another pack of Marlboros from her backpack and slipped out the door. *Gelato actually does sound good*, she reasoned, especially considering her dessert had been stolen. Walking alone through the narrow flagstone streets at night felt liberating. The rich aroma of stewed and roasted meat still sat low in the cool air. The teenagers were still congregating in the plaza and a few tourists remained sitting cross legged at their tables, lovingly gazing into their partner's eyes, drunk off cheap island wine. She stopped into a small ice cream parlor and asked for a cup of lemon sorbet, which she then took outside and savored slowly while meandering through the town. On an empty street, she saw a tabby cat sleeping under a wooden folding sign with a slogan written in chalk: *Delicious Food for Delicious People*. Behind the low stone wall next to the sign was a quaint tavern with a long picnic bench in the courtyard full of people laughing and drinking bottled beer. She turned her head in a moment of curiosity and immediately, almost psychically, made eye contact with Cherry. She leaped up from the bench, her cheeks rosy from the alcohol and, with an ecstatic smile, beelined to Marissa.

"Hey! Marissa, right? Where's the boyfriend?"

"He's passed out in the room."

"Had a bit too much, eh? You alone then?"

"Yeah. Just taking a little night walk."

"Join us! Have a beer!"

"That's okay. I don't want to impose."

"What are you talking about? I just invited you. Come on," she playfully grabbed Marissa's arm and brought her to the table. "Hey Gang," she interrupted the table's conversation. "This is Marissa. We met on the ferry the other day. Marissa, this is the gang. That's Tom. Next to him, his boyfriend David. Rob, Danny, Marcus, Isaac and Charlie," they all nodded cordially.

"You want a beer?" asked one of the guys. She couldn't remember his name.

"Sure," she replied sheepishly.

"Great. Another round then for the table?"

"Yes please!" Tom smiled at his friend. Marissa recognized him as the guy from Mexico who had interrogated the retired couple.

"Scoot over. Make some room," commanded Cherry, and the

guys nestled closer together so Marissa could sit. She planted herself next to Cherry, opened her pack of cigarettes and offered some to the table. Two of the guys accepted one and they took turns lighting them with her Bic before handing it back to her so she could do the same.

"So Marissa - Where're you from?" asked the guy across from her. *Was he Rob?* She thought, but figured it didn't matter as long as she was friendly.

"I live in New York but I was raised in San Diego."

"You know how to surf?" asked David.

"I'm not very good at it. I'm more of a read-on-the-beach type of girl."

"But you do know how?" he asked again.

"I took some lessons one summer. I stood up on the wave a few times."

"Cherry here was almost a pro, you know?" said the guy sitting next to her. *Was he Marcus?*

The guy who had been sitting across from Tom came back holding nine beer bottles with both hands. He distributed them and one of the guys said "Thanks Charlie".

"Almost a pro?" Marissa asked, turning to Cherry, feeling more at home as her cigarette burned.

"I've been at it all my life. It's pretty big in Perth. I decided to stop one day after I was out with my older brother and he got bit by a shark," she said, her accent producing a tingling comfort around the crown of Marissa's head.

"Is he alright?" she asked. Smaller conversations picked up around the table. They'd all heard the story before.

"Yeah. He's fine. Just took a little chunk out of his thigh. He was back out there a few weeks later. But it was enough of a scare for me to stay on dry land," she said nonchalantly, then sipped her beer.

"You know," said the guy next to her, "One in five people who surf in Australia have been attacked by sharks."

"That's such a load of shit, Marcus," Cherry laughed.

"So you guys are all here on a friend's trip together?" Marissa tried changing the subject.

"Basically," said Marcus. "Most of us work remotely and Cherry here is taking two years and traveling the world so we just had to coordinate around Tom and David's schedule."

"And how'd you all meet?" she asked Marcus.

Marissa lit another cigarette.

"Well, Danny and I've known each other since we were kids. We met Rob and Charlie at uni in london. Tom and David were Rob's friends at first and Isaac and Charlie used to hook up. They're just friends now. We met Cherry in Vietnam a year ago and since then, we've all been in the group chat figuring out where to go next."

"That's so cool. God. It would be so great to have a big group of friends like you guys."

"What are you talking about? You do now, Love. Cheers," Marcus said warmly, lifting his bottle.

"Cheers!" Marissa smiled.

The festivity continued until the man who ran the tavern told them he had to go home to his wife. It had been two and a half hours and probably four beers each. After giving out cigarettes like halloween candy, Marissa had four left in her pack. She felt lightheaded when she stood and Cherry grabbed her arm to stabilize her. Tom and David said goodnight and split off from the group to

group got closer to finishing the second bottle of vodka, the women's comments became more and more ignored. Cherry suggested she return to her hotel and suggested Marissa join her downstairs for another cigarette. Marissa to check the time on her phone. Almost four. They guys drunkenly said goodnight and the girls went downstairs.

The moon raced across the sky and hid behind the hillside monastery, casting the town in shadow. Cherry pulled the weathered pack of Touch Blues from her jacket pocket, offered one to Marissa and lit it for her. The lighter's yellow flame reflected in Cherry's irises, and her pupil looked like a small rounded obsidian in a bed of gold dust. She wrapped the burgundy scarf over her head and asked for a drag of the cigarette.

"Why don't you come up to my room and we share one more drink?" Cherry suggested.

"It's not too far, right?"

"Just a few minutes away,"

Cherry's hotel was probably the most quaint in the entire town. Her room key unlocked the front door, and they turned a corner to a room on the ground floor. The building had previously been a single family home but was remodeled to accommodate guests. In the room stood a small wooden desk against the wall and over it hung a painting of a sunset. At the desk was a matching wooden chair and against the opposite wall was a bed which occupied most of the room. Marissa pulled the chair from the desk and sat down. She asked Cherry for a glass of water and noticed the nightstand had a jewelry tray full of oversized colorful earrings. Beside the tray was an unopened bottle of ouzo. Probably complimentary. Cherry filled a glass with tap water from the restroom sink and handed it to Marissa. She took a sip, then looked across the room at Cherry as she took out her earrings and placed them gently in the tray.

"Ouzo's good for you? It's all I've got," said Cherry.

"Perfect. Thanks," Marissa replied.

"Mind if I get more comfortable?" she said, already taking off her shoes.

"Of course not."

Cherry turned on a lamp beside the bed then clicked the switch by the door, turning off the overhead light.

"There aren't any shot glasses, so we can just share the bottle," said Cherry, taking off her jacket. "Come sit on the bed. It's way more comfy than that chair."

Marissa slid off her sneakers and sat at the edge of the bed, facing the window. The golden streetlight cast a thick shadow of a flowering bougainvillea branch on the wall across the street. Marissa felt Cherry's fingers gently run through her hair, exposing the side of her neck. As quickly as she started to turn, Cherry was kissing the back of her shoulder where it met her neck. Marissa moaned softly. Cherry continued up her neck, making her way just behind her ear. Marissa twisted her body, grabbed Cherry's waist and their lips met.

They kissed for a full minute before undressing rapidly, maintaining eye contact the whole time. With their clothes strewn about the floor beside the bed, they embraced each other and continued a long sensuous kiss before falling to their sides, their heads resting on the pillows. Marissa felt Cherry's hand caress the side of her face then further down as her kisses moved to her neck, then her breasts and down her torso. She threw her head back in ecstasy when

Cherry's hands gently brushed her inner thighs. She relaxed her body and felt time beginning to stand still. Closing her eyes, she could vividly recall the evening's sunset. In her memory, she felt the warmth of the evening's starlight, as though each star had lived and died and exploded, every supernova existing only for her.

She opened her eyes to find Cherry's back arched, her tiger eyes fixed on her own, like a big cat stalking prey through the veldt. Marissa leaned forward and embraced her, kissing her softly then gently flipping her onto her back and clumsily reciprocating the pleasure.

CHAPTER EIGHT

A pale lavender dawn spread over the island. The shadow of the bougainvillea faded away in the morning light. The two women lay next to each other, wearing only a thin veneer of tender sunlight. Cherry's balayage blonde hair, previously tucked away in the piercing rain on the ferry, now rested freely on a soft down pillow and tickled Marissa's arm. *Her body is immaculate*, Marissa thought, taking her in. Ivory skin, well proportioned shoulders, soft peach colored nipples... Like the memory of her own nude body in the mirror in Athens.

"Fuck," she said, sitting up sharply as if she'd just stepped on an electric eel. Marissa swung her feet over the side of the bed and started putting on her socks.

"The boyfriend..." Cherry said, bringing her hand to her forehead.

"Fuck. Fuck. Fuck," Marissa repeated, frantically putting on her clothes. "I'm really sorry but I, like, really have to go."

"Yeah. Totally. I wouldn't want to get you in trouble."

"I had a really great time though. I really wish I could stay."

"It's totally fine. Really. I had a nice time too."

"Oh. Fuck," Marissa sighed, fully dressed and surveying the room to see if she'd missed anything. Cherry got up and kissed her on the cheek. Her butt bounced firmly as she walked to the bathroom to brush her teeth. Marissa stood watching her like a deer in headlights.

"Go! He's gonna wake up, yeah?" said Cherry, her mouth full of toothpaste.

Marissa closed the door behind her as she left and stepped into the morning air. It still carried the night's chill. The periwinkle sky was brightening by the minute and when she turned to glance back into the window to see the room where she'd spent the early hours, the curtain was drawn. She jogged back to the resort and let herself into the room with her card key.

Zack was still exactly where he had collapsed earlier, lying diagonally on the bed under a single blanket. Marissa moved silently across the room then flipped up the sheets on the edge bed and turned the pillow slightly. She kicked off her shoes, and locked herself in the bathroom. She took a look in the mirror. Her eyes looked heavy and her lips had a faint blue stain around the edges. After a long shower and a full five minutes brushing her teeth, she felt slightly refreshed but still exhausted. When she stepped out of the bathroom in a robe and a towel wrapped around her hair, the day's light was filtering into the room through the sheer white curtains and Zack was sitting up in bed with his phone in his hand.

"Hey, Babe. Good morning," he said, setting his phone on the nightstand. "I'm sorry about last night. I probably had a bit too much to drink."

"It's no problem. Good morning," she replied.

"I don't know. I feel bad about it. I don't know what came over me."

"Really, it's not a big deal," Marissa searched her backpack for a clean set of underwear.

"Think you could grab me a glass of water?"

"Sure. One sec," she stepped into her panties then filled a glass from the bathroom tap. He flung his legs over the edge of the bed as she handed it to him. As he gulped it down, she yawned quietly. She would have loved to crawl in bed and sleep for ten hours.

Once they'd gotten dressed and had coffee in the room, they headed downstairs to the lobby for breakfast. Zack piled his plate with eggs, bacon and three fried cheese pies. Marissa had some fruit and a cappuccino. She was too tired to engage in conversation, so when Zack suggested ideas for the day's activities, she just nodded along and said she'd be okay with whatever he wanted to do. After breakfast, they returned to the room and Marissa had a cigarette and another espresso on the patio while Zack showered. She could hear children laughing in the town and birds singing their morning songs.

"You have your swimsuit on?" Zack called out from across the room.

"Huh?" she replied from the balcony.

"Your bathing suit. You going to use one?"

"Yeah. I forgot. I'll put it on in a minute."

"You don't need to if you don't want to," he said, pulling out the chair next to her then sitting and helping himself to one of her Marlboros. She grabbed a second one and he lit it for her. She stared across the low white rooftops at the silver ocean on the horizon. She would certainly have been asleep if not for the three shots of espresso.

"You can just go nude if you want," he said.

"What?"

"To the beach. You don't have to bring your swimsuit if you

don't want to."

"No. I'll bring it. Just give me a minute. I'll change."

She put out her cigarette after a few more drags then went inside and put on a small brown bikini. He'd picked it for her, saying it matched her hair. Over it, she put on a long black skirt and a white tank top and an olive green cardigan. Zack was wearing blue board shorts and a yellow cable knit Polo sweater. They both grabbed their sunglasses and stepped into their matching Birkenstocks. Zack grabbed the beach bag and stuffed it with towels and books. They closed the door to the room and made sure it was locked then strolled over to the closest ATV rental office.

A middle aged couple with matching tan complexions ran the little store. Outside, there were four ATVs parked next to each other and inside was a wall of helmets. Zack paid in cash to get the discounted rate. Fifty euro for the day. Then the man helped them find helmets that fit and explained how the vehicle operated. The tank was almost empty, so they pulled into a gas station next to the rental shop where a twelve year old boy filled their ATV with twenty euros of diesel. They sped along the island's only road to the northern end and felt the wind ruffle their clothes.. High on the center of the island, they pulled over to take in the view. Across the calm Aegean, they could see all the other islands. Sikinos to the east, Paros and Antiparos to the north, Sifnos to the northwest and at the edge of the horizon was Milos. Zack pointed to it.

"We were just there," he said.

The sky was clear and cloudless and from the top of the ridge, their view stretched for miles. Zack pointed to the nearby eastern island.

"That's where we're going next."

"That's cool," Marissa yawned.

They continued up the road to the village of Ano Meria where they stopped at a small roadside café to buy snacks and cigarettes. An old man wearing a stained white linen shirt and tan trousers was drinking a Greek coffee and smoking a cigarillo at the dark corner table. Marissa noticed he was missing a hand. With their supplies replenished, they continued on, passing an isolated church, then turned down a dirt road. Marissa straddled Zack as he whipped the ATV around the corners of the steep downhill path. It took ten minutes to reach sea level and Zack parked at the second beach they found. The white sand stretched the length of a football pitch and was flanked by rocks at one end. At the other was an abandoned line of houses built into the cliffside and a similarly abandoned concrete dock. They set their towels on the sand and Zack threw off his clothes and dashed nude into the clear water. Even in October, the warm sun felt comfortable on Marissa's skin. Not too hot and not too cold, absolutely perfect. She slid off her skirt and pulled the tank top over her head and folded them neatly next to her. She tried reading for a minute then set the book down and fell asleep.

When Zack was six years old, his mother had enrolled him in swimming classes at the community pool. By the end of the course, the children were made to race each other from one end of the pool to the other. Zack won. His pride in this led him to be the captain of his middle school swim club and eventually the captain of his high school competitive team. His childhood bedroom was filled with trophies from various meets. When he got to college, he tried to join the swim team but was humbled by the other applicants. If he couldn't be a big fish in a small pond, he figured there was no point in racing. He still swam at the school gym but felt no need for competition. Swimming for him became not only a form of stress relief, but an outlet for his sexuality. He'd notice every college girl wearing goggles, a swim cap, and a skin tight one piece and he'd mentally picture them stripping off in the locker room and showering as a group. And so, Zack developed a swimsuit fetish. It wasn't the swimsuits themselves that turned him on, but the inevitability of their removal.

His mind was both empty and occupied as he swam aimlessly that morning. The sun felt good on his cheeks and his muscles moved with the sea's current. He thought about Marissa taking off her bikini and just how good her body would look on an empty beach. He pictured it in his mind - his girlfriend standing naked on the white sand, with the calm sea behind her and a crystal clear sky. The light shining in her green eyes and her brunette hair made wavy by the surf - the light patch of pubic hair being her only adornment. She was nature, just as he was. What could be more natural than a couple in love, undisturbed and disrobed, embraced by the sea at the edge of the world?

He stepped out of the water and returned to his towel to find Marissa asleep, lying face down on her stomach. Not wanting to disturb her, he quietly reached into the beach bag to find sunscreen and grab his book. He was about half way into *Diamonds are Forever* and James Bond was just arriving in Las Vegas. He got bored after a chapter and grabbed his phone. America was asleep. Nothing to do. Nobody to talk to. Sitting on a windless warm beach at the bottom of a cliff, his girlfriend asleep next to him, and with a clear view of any coming vehicles on the only road down the mountain, he searched for some porn and quietly masturbated. Marissa showed no sign of waking up. When he finished, he ate an orange and smoked a Marlboro Red from a newly purchased pack, then jumped back in the water for a twenty minute swim.

Returning to his towel the second time, he felt fatigued and his stomach was growling. He looked at his Omega Seamaster and watched a full circumgyration of the second hand, both appreciating the timepiece and utterly bored. The boredom led to restlessness and he gently touched Marissa's shoulder to wake her. She wiped a bit of drool from her lip and turned to him.

"Hey Babe. You've been napping a while and I didn't want you to burn," he lied. He just wanted company.

"How long was I out?"

"About an hour and a half."

"Just a little more," she said weakly, collapsing back into her prone position.

"Babe. Let me put some sunscreen on you."

"Fine," she said, twisting her body and propping herself up.

He rubbed her shoulders and back and then asked her to return the favor. She applied the sunscreen to his skin, returning the favor, then rubbed the excess from her hands into her arms. A full sized SUV was rolling slowly down the steep dirt road to the beach and upon seeing it, Zack suggested they leave for an early lunch. Marissa didn't object so he slid back on his swim trunks and packed the beach bag. Marissa stepped back into her skirt then they tossed the bag in the ATV's luggage tray and headed up the mountain.

He has no idea, she thought, straddling him as he labored to steer. *Would he even be mad if he knew?*

The diesel engine vibrated for another twenty minutes and after another road down to sea level, they arrived at Agkali - a small cove, with a spattering of hotels and restaurants. They parked in the dirt and walked up a paved cliffside path to a tavern overlooking the sea. They sat outside and the waiter brought them menus and a carafe of water. The daily special was ladenia, a pie made with tomato and onion. They ordered two pieces of it and a greek salad. It was too early for wine. While they shared the salad, a light breeze flew in from the west and small white clouds formed on the horizon. They finished the pies (which more resembled focaccia) then paid their bill and continued up the path. It was a fifteen minute walk along the edge of a cliff to reach Paralia Agios Nikolaos. Once they turned the corner to see the gray sand lining a perfectly calm inlet flanked by a grove of olive trees, they noticed about ten other people on the beach, all completely nude. Marissa politely made an effort not to look at any of them.

They picked a spot under an olive tree near the far end of the beach. Zack immediately stripped after setting down his towel, then declared he was going to walk around and find the best place to enter the water. He strutted around on the wet sand, showing off his swimmer's body then eased himself into the water at the opposite side of the cove. The breeze strengthened into a gentle wind and some clouds started rolling fast across the sky so Marissa grabbed her cardigan from the bag and put it on. She took off her sunglasses and read another chapter of *A Wild Sheep Chase* while Zack swam.

"Marissa?" came a voice from a few yards away. She turned to see two skinny nude men, both in sunglasses looking towards her. One of them lowered their shades and she recognized them. It was Tom and David.

"Hey," she said apprehensively, putting down her book.

"So that's the boyfriend?" Tom asked, turning his head towards the sea.

Zack was the only one swimming.

"Yeah. That's Zack."

"Why didn't we meet him last night?" asked David. "He's cute."

"He was passed out in the room."

"Why don't you two join us tonight for drinks again?" suggested Tom.

"I think we have plans tonight, but I appreciate the invitation."

"Que lastima. Es guapo, ¿no?" Tom said to David.

"He's giving trade," David agreed.

"Are any of the others coming here to join you guys?" Marissa asked.

"No, Honey. Just us. I think the gang's still asleep," said David.

"They're all nocturnal," Tom chimed in.

Zack emerged dripping from the sea and walked the length of the sand before sitting next to Marissa on his towel. His lean muscles were aching from the tugging of the current and from piloting the ATV but he felt youthful and alive. During his swim, light gray clouds had rolled in from over the southern bluff that wrapped the inlet. A slight drizzle of rain, barely detectable, fell onto the sand and a few of the old couples put on their clothes and started their way back up the path to the parking lot before it got colder. Tom and David also got dressed and packed up their things then waved and said "Bye Hon," to

Marissa before beginning their trek back to Chora.

"Do you know those guys?" Zack asked, toweling his hair.

"Just met them. They're nice."

"That's cool. Where're they from?"

"I didn't think to ask."

"Hmm..."

Zack grabbed a Marlboro Red from the beach bag and offered one to Marissa. He lit her cigarette then lit his. Looking down at her cigarette, Marissa noticed tiny droplets of water polka dotting the white paper. Zack asked Marissa if she wanted to "make love under the olive trees" and she politely declined, citing the weather.

They were walking back along the cliffside path when the rain strengthened from a mist to a sprinkling. It would still be a while before the ground turned muddy, so they took their time and appreciated the view of the endless cerulean expanse before them. Halfway along the path, Marissa noticed the one-handed old man she'd seen earlier. In his right and only hand was a pickaxe and the stump of his left hand was stabilizing the handle as he swung into the hillside to widen the path. With each swing, fragments of loose earth fell onto the path and he compressed them with his boot. She said hello to him and, without answering in words, he looked up at her and nodded.

CHAPTER NINE

From the shelter of a beachside café in Agkali, Marissa heard the roaring crash of massive waves as the wind howled and torrents of rain poured down, striking the patio's fabric canopy and occasionally dripping through onto her shoulder. The storm had moved in from the south and didn't take long to enshroud Folegandros. Zack was inside ordering Greek coffees and buying a pack of cigarillos. At a table across the patio, a middle aged German couple was playing backgammon while they slowly drank a bottle of white wine.

"The guy inside said the rain will probably stop in half an hour," Zack announced, returning to the table with the coffees.

"That's good," Marissa was shivering a little.

Zack grabbed a blanket that was draped over one of the chairs and covered Marissa's shoulders before kissing her on the forehead.

"Well, it won't fully stop completely. But it should subside enough for us to get back to Chora without getting soaked."

"There's no rush. It's nice here."

"Well, I don't want you to get sick. After this we should take a hot shower together. Maybe get in the hot tub at the resort?"

Although Marissa did think that sounded lovely, she knew that he was speaking in code and he really wanted sex. And while she would usually be happy to satisfy his craving, she was tired and fighting off pangs of quiet guilt.

"Yeah. Okay," she said acceptingly.

"Are you okay?" he asked, sitting next to her and wrapping his arm around her shoulder.

"Yeah. I'm fine," she looked up at him and smiled.

"You sure? You don't seem like yourself today."

"Maybe I'm just tired. We've been moving around a lot. Like, I'm having a really nice time. It's just, this feels more like an adventure than a vacation."

"That's exactly what this is. We're on an adventure in the Greek islands. And yeah, I guess October wasn't the best month to come here. It was a lot cheaper than coming in the summer though. And I bet a lot emptier too. I feel like it would be a lot worse to come here and be surrounded by influencers and Russian whores. I'd much rather have peace even if it comes with a little bit of rain. When the storm lets up, let's head back to the hotel and just take it easy. I don't want you to feel drained."

Marissa grabbed a cigarette from the beach bag.

"I love you," she said.

"I love you too Babe," he leaned over to kiss her, then unwrapped the pack of cigarillos and lit one.

It took almost an hour for the downpour to become tolerable enough for a twenty minute ATV ride. In that time, they each drank two Greek coffees, smoked four cigarettes and played a game of chess. Marissa was completely exhausted by the time they returned to the room and Zack suggested they soak in the hot tub while they still had their swimsuits on and while it was still raining. Fueled by caffeine, she agreed. They dropped their bag in their room then walked down to the courtyard. They were the only guests at the resort - typical for October in the middle of the week. Lowering their shoulders into the hot water, they felt the raindrops bounce off the surface and the steam relax their muscles.

"God. I needed this," Zack declared softly, closing his eyes and sinking further into the water.

Marissa felt the rain hit her forehead and could hear each beat of her heart. She looked up at the muted gray sky. Her heart started beating faster and she began to feel lightheaded. She lifted herself out of the tub to sit on the edge. As she did, her body trembled and her vision went black. Her arms lost their strength, failed to support her, and she collapsed on her side. Her shoulder hit the concrete first, preventing her skull from taking the hit.

"Oh fuck! Marissa! Are you okay?" Zack leaped from the water. "Marissa!?"

The young receptionist in the lobby noticed and rushed out with a towel and a glass of water. Zack leaned her up against his body and she immediately regained consciousness. He thanked the receptionist and covered Marissa with the towel and asked her to drink slowly when she felt like she could.

"I'm fine," Marissa insisted.

"You just had a seizure," he said.

"It happens. I'm fine."

"Babe. You're not fine. That's scary as fuck. Maybe we should find a doctor."

"I'm fine. Really. I just haven't had enough water today," she said weakly. She couldn't tell if her skin was wet with sweat, rain, or the hot tub water.

"Okay, well, drink this," he said, handing her the water.

"The town doctor is in Ano Meria. I can call him if you'd like," said the receptionist.

"No. No. I'm fine. Really," Marissa pleaded.

"I think she'll be okay," said Zack. "Slowly Babe," he said, helping her hold the water cup.

Once she'd recovered enough, they walked back up to the room and Marissa insisted on taking a nap. Zack was apprehensive but could do nothing to stop her from crawling under the blanket and falling asleep. He took a quick shower and by the time he got out, she was snoring. He drew the curtains, put on some clean clothes then wrote a quick note explaining he'd gone for a walk and left it beside her on the nightstand.

The stone streets of Chora were empty in the rain. Not a single person or cat was about. Letting himself get soaked, Zack walked to the opposite edge of town to the vista point at the foot of the hill leading to the monastery. Standing at the top of a two hundred meter cliff, the stormy sea looked calm, completely unlike the waves at Agkali. Shrouded by mist in the distance was the outline of Sikinos, the next island they were scheduled to visit. He stood in the rain for five minutes, staring out at the sea. The water had penetrated his hair and he could feel the cool droplets running down his scalp. He continued walking circularly through the town and the rain slowly eased to a stop. He heard little brown buntings chirping, sheltered under the magenta flowers of the bougainvillea branches, celebrating the storm's end and their forthcoming feast of ants, impatiently enticed to the surface to collect water. The sun, falling to meet the horizon, peaked out from the rolling clouds and soft amber light shone through the windows of the white houses, their walls taking on a lavender hue as the fleeting daylight retreated behind the mist, casting twilight in a faint kaleidoscopic glow through the flowers like stained glass. Though still too early for dinner, the aroma of stewed goat wafted over the town and clung to the moist air. *I should get her some food*, he thought. Apart from his concern for Marissa, Zack's mind was trouble free. Everything was going well at work. His friends were all fine. His sister was expecting her first child and the thrill of that had helped his mom quickly get over her divorce. Overall, his family was happy. He was happy. Even his dad was happy on his island with his new girlfriend.

Zack stopped into the only restaurant in the town open in the late afternoon and ordered two gyros to go. He took them back to the hotel room and found Marissa still sleeping. He ate his sandwich, then picked up his book and read half a chapter before putting the bookmark in the page and taking out his phone to look at porn.

Marissa woke up an hour later. The room's heater was turned on and Zack was lying in bed next to her. He put his phone on the nightstand when he noticed she'd woken up.

"Hey Babe. I got you a gyro. Are you feeling a little better? Want some water?" he asked attentively.

"That's sweet. Thank you," she said, stepping out of bed.

She hadn't taken off her bikini and the bed was wet where she had slept. She felt itchy from the chlorine and salt water but she was also starving. She inhaled the gyro then took a long hot shower. In this interval, Zack looked at more porn, got bored and smoked a cigarillo while standing on the balcony. The sun had set and the rooftops melded together in the cloud diffused moonlight. After a few minutes outside, Zack saw the town's soft yellow street lights turn on simultaneously. He put out his cigarillo when he heard the shower faucet turn off and came back inside. A few minutes later, Marissa dried herself and emerged from the steamed bathroom wrapped in her robe and towel.

"I don't know about you, but I'm still pretty hungry. I was thinking we could take the ATV to the port and grab dinner there. We should get fish again," Zack proposed, watching as Marissa rummaged through her backpack for a clean outfit.

"Sure. That sounds good. I'm sorry about earlier."

"For what?"

"Almost dying on you."

"Baby. You don't have to apologize for almost dying. It's probably my fault anyway. I should have brought water with us to the beach."

"It's not your fault. I could have brought some too."

"Yeah. But when you're with me, I feel like I should be taking care of you. It makes me happy to make you happy."

Marissa stepped into a clean pair of panties without taking off her bathrobe.

"Let's go out for a bottle of wine and some snacks before dinner," Zack suggested.

"You sure you'll be okay to drive after half a bottle?"

"It'll be fine. I won't get drunk like last night."

"Maybe I can drive us," Marissa said, drying her hair.

"It's not so easy to drive that thing. It doesn't have power steering. Every turn is a workout."

"Are you saying I can't do it?"

"Well, no but..."

"Have you ever tried walking seven Bullmastiffs at the same time?"

"It's a little different. They listen to you."

"I'm strong. I can drive the ATV."

"Well if you want to, you can, but..."

"But what?"

"But I'd prefer it if you didn't. I mean, you did just have a little seizure earlier."

"Just don't drink too much then," she said, putting on a maroon t-shirt, tight gray jeans and her denim jacket.

They put on their shoes and walked around Chora. A few other couples were sitting near the plaza and the teenagers had come out again in what appeared to be a nightly ritual. They sat down outside a tavern in the plaza and ordered two glasses of red wine along with a plate of dolmadakia. They ate their stuffed grape leaves and drank slowly, enjoying the calm night air. After the storm had passed, the whole island felt warmer as if the rain had restored its internal energy. While sipping his wine, Zack noticed a small group of people around his age walking through the plaza and his vision beelined to a blonde woman wearing a black leather jacket and oversized yellow flower earrings. He stared long enough for Marissa to wonder what he was looking at and she turned to see. Cherry and the gang. She turned back and took a sip of her wine.

"I think those are the two guys you were talking to at the beach today," said Zack.

"Oh, really? It's a small island."

"I can't really tell for sure though. You know, the receptionist told me yesterday that there are only five hundred people living here."

"Really?"

"Yeah. Could you imagine? Living in a place like this? I sort of wish we could just live on a little island and live a peaceful life."

"We *do* live on an island and I'd say our life is pretty peaceful."

"What are you talking about?"

"Manhattan's an island."

Zack laughed.

"You know what I mean," he said.

They paid the bill and walked to the dirt lot where they'd left the ATV. Ten minutes later, after driving south down the island's only road, they parked by the port and entered a small restaurant. An old couple were the only people working there and there was one other couple, middle-aged Americans finishing an early dinner. They grabbed a table on the terrace by the road and a silent drizzle of rain, only visible under the streetlamp, came to keep them company. After a few minutes, the woman who owned the restaurant came to take their order. Her gray hair was tied back in a ponytail and she wore a stained white apron over a long sun faded dress. Her husband was enjoying a cigarillo and an espresso at a small table across from them. Zack ordered a bottle of white wine, fried sardines, stuffed squid, and a sea bream grilled whole. The woman smiled and thanked them for their order then turned to her husband and spoke sharply at him in Greek, prompting him to return inside and help prepare the food. A minute later, the old man came to the table with two glasses and the bottle. His hands looked strong and his skin shined tightly over his muscles, betraying his age. He uncorked it and poured the glasses almost full.

"What time are we leaving tomorrow?" asked Marissa.

"The ferry departs at ten, so we should probably check out before nine and just hang out around here for an hour. The hotel driver can take us so we don't have to walk. I'll return the ATV tonight. They're so chill there. They said just park it where it was and leave the key in the ignition. They always keep the door unlocked too. You know how many police officers they have on this island? Two."

"What do they do if somebody commits a crime?" Marrisa lit a cigarette.

"Well they generally don't here. But I suppose if they did, they'd be handcuffed and processed and sent to the capital to be jailed."

"In Athens?"

"No. The capital of the Cyclades is Ermoupoli. In Syros. We're going there after Santorini."

"How long are we going to be there for?"

"Syros or Santorini?"

"Santorini."

"Just two nights. I couldn't get a good deal on the hotel."

"It's not like you to be so frugal," she said before taking a sip of wine. It was dry and taut.

"Yes it is. What are you talking about? I always try to save money where I can."

"You just ordered a sixty five dollar fish," Marissa puffed on her Marlboro Red, sending a tendril of pale smoke upward.

"There are two things in life that you should never try to save money on. One is jewelry and the other is food."

"Oh yeah? Where'd you steal that line from?"

"I didn't."

"Well, I'm not complaining."

69

The old man came with the tray of sardines and the stuffed squid. He refilled their glasses after placing silverware on the table.

"I come back with bread," he said.

"Efcharistó," Marissa said, thanking him.

"Parakalo," he replied.

By the time the bream arrived butterflied on a platter, they'd finished the bottle of wine and Zack ordered a second. The soft rain continued and Zack spent the rest of the meal talking about work while Marissa pretended to listen. She had become adept at zoning him out and replying as though she was paying attention. She ended up eating more than half of the fish while he drank more than his share of the bottle. For dessert, they ordered yogurt and honey. Marissa made sure to eat it quickly. The old man brought them two shot glasses and poured them each a shot of limoncello.

"On the house," he said.

"Thank you so much. Everything was delicious," said Zack. He downed his shot and sat back in his wooden chair with a blissful grin plastered on his face.

"You can have mine if you want," Marissa offered.

"You sure?"

"Yeah. I don't like limoncello," she lied.

"Who doesn't like limoncello?" he said. He grabbed her shot glass and downed it rapidly before exhaling.

Marissa noticed the veins in his hand as he reached across the table. That was one of the things she found most attractive about him. But somehow, her mind was drifting to Cherry again. The contrast between his hairy muscled fingers and her delicate maroon manicure. His hard toned swimmer's body and her supple soft skin. She was

70

staring blankly at the rain dancing in the ocean breeze under the streetlamp like gold flakes falling through clear liquor. However, in her mind, she was visualizing what it would look like if Zack and Cherry made love.

"You good?" Zack asked.

Marissa snapped back into reality.

"Yeah. All good."

"Were you zoning out?"

"A little," she sipped her wine.

"You're so cute. I'm gonna find the bathroom then get the check."

"Let me get this one. You've been paying for everything."

"You sure?"

"Yeah. It's my turn."

"Thanks Babe," he said. He took a moment after standing up to stabilize himself, then sauntered inside.

Marissa was surprisingly sober. She'd eaten most of the bread with olive oil and didn't stop when a second basket was served with the fish. The old man was having another coffee and smoking outside at his table when Marissa turned and made eye contact with him. He understood she wanted to pay the bill and he stepped inside behind a low counter with an old cash register on it. She followed him in. There were sunbleached photographs taped to the wall behind him. One of them caught her eye - a depiction of him as a young man. He was sitting on a wooden boat, holding a fish. His skin was burnt dark by the sun and his musculature was that which could only be forged by ocean waves. His beard was dark and thick and his similarly dark eyes shone exceedingly clearly. She guessed he must have been in his mid-thirties in the photo. He smiled proudly when he saw her examine it, appreciating the gifts bestowed upon him by the sea.

CHAPTER TEN

The road leading up from the port was damp and unlit. Marissa drove slowly while Zack clinged onto her. Rain continued to fall as mist. The yellow lights of Chora glowed through the fog in the distance. She parked the ATV in the communal lot and they returned to their room.

"What do you think? Should we make love?" Zack asked, half drunk and half joking.

Marissa rolled her eyes.

"Yeah. Okay. Let me hit the bathroom first though."

Zack wanted a cigarette but thought that if he opened the door to the balcony, he'd let in the cold and Marissa would be less inclined to take her clothes off. On many occasions, she would leave her shirt on while they had sex and though he didn't complain, he always felt the urge to remove it. What he did not know is that Marissa would leave it on as an invitation for him to undress her. He was too polite to realize this and she was too coy to demand it.

She left her shirt on.

Seven minutes later, they shared a cigarette on the balcony then retired to the bed to read. James Bond was playing blackjack at Tiffany Case's table and the narrator of the Murakami novel was wandering around Hokkaido, looking for a clue as to the location of the sheep.

Marissa devoured the words, thoroughly engrossed in the story when she heard Zack snoring. He fell asleep with the book half opened on his chest. After two more chapters, she placed both their books on the nightstand and turned off the lights. He was still snoring. Very carefully, she got up from the bed and put her clothes back on, including her denim jacket. She made sure she had her card key then quietly slipped out the door.

In the town, the lamplight reflected off the street's wet stones and white lime veins, painting them teal and gold. The plaza's activity was exactly that as the night before, as though every day was the same on the island. Marissa was starting to miss the sounds of the city. She missed the energy. She was walking aimlessly through the small town with one singular goal - to find Cherry. First she walked past the tavern where she'd seen her, then past the place where they'd had beers. No luck. She wandered through the mist for almost an hour, taking the same paths two or three times and moving slowly to look into the windows of the few open restaurants. She wondered what she would do if she found her. She walked past her hotel room and the light was out, then walked past the other hotel where the guys were staying and saw no lights on there. She stopped at the vista point at the edge of the town to light another cigarette. The Aegean two hundred meters below her was lacquered black like a freshly paved road. Almost no light penetrated the cloud cover. As she was about to give up and return to the room, she heard a distant but familiar laugh from up on the hill. It sounded uproarious and gay and she knew it was the gang. She started up the winding path to the monastery. The laughter intensified in volume as she grew closer. She found them sitting on an outcrop of rocks about two thirds the way up the hillside path.

"Eyy, look who found us!" said Isaac.

"Marissa!" Marcus cheered.

"Hey guys," she said.

"What are you doing up here?" Cherry asked, not confrontationally but feigning warmth.

"I was just out for a night walk and I heard you guys laughing up here so I thought I'd see if I could hang out a little."

"Oh my God. Are we really that loud? You heard us from down there?" asked Danny. He made no effort to be quieter.

"You're probably not bothering anybody," she reassured him.

"Join us Hun," said Marcus. "I'll trade you a beer for a cigarette. Oh, be careful. The rocks are slippery."

She found a rock to sit on and handed Marcus a cigarette.

"Where's the rest of the group?" Marissa asked.

"Tom and David are taking the night ferry to Santorini and Rob and Charlie are off somewhere doing God knows what," Danny said.

"I could take a guess," laughed Isaac.

"What was I saying? Oh! Greg Kinnear. For sure," Marcus said.

"Yes. Definitely. He's got such warm eyes," Danny agreed.

"I think Mads Mikkelsen's pretty hot," said Cherry, exhaling smoke from her Touch Blue.

"You *would* think that," Danny said, mockingly.

"I've got one. Ralph Fiennes," Isaac interjected.

"Are you fucking serious Isaac? You'd fuck voldemort?" Marcus asked.

"First of all, who wouldn't? Second, he just got fucking shredded for some new movie," Isaac defended his assertion.

"Okay but *Schnidler's List* though? He was hideous in that!" said

Marcus.

"He was not. And if you think that, it's only because he was a Nazi," said Isaac.

"Your turn Marissa. Who's your favorite silver fox?" Danny asked, politely inviting her into the conversation.

"Oh. I feel so put on the spot. I don't know. Who's the guy from *In the Mood for Love*? Does he count?"

"Yes. Yes. Yes. What's his name? But one hundred percent yes," said Marcus.

"Tony Leung," Danny replied.

"So you're a film buff?" asked Isaac.

"I don't know. I guess," Marissa lit a cigarette.

"No need to be shy about it," said Cherry.

"Tony's such a sexy name," declared Marcus.

"Really? I don't know. I just think Tony Soprano," said Isaac.

"Like he isn't sexy. Italian names are just hot in general," Marcus said. "Luca, Fabrizio, Nico, Antonio..."

"It's only because you're not Italian you think that," Danny joked.

"Okay. As if you don't think Italians are hot," Marcus took a sip of his beer.

"Marissa, what's your boyfriend's name? And where is he?" asked Isaac.

Cherry turned to Marissa.

"Zack. He's sleeping."

"Oh. That's an unfortunate name," said Danny.

"Don't be mean!" Isaac laughed.

"No. I'm sorry. I didn't mean it like that. I actually have an uncle in America named Zack. You know it's a Hebrew name? It means God remembers," said Danny.

"What's my name mean?" asked Marcus.

"Roman. Sworn to Mars, the God of war," Danny didn't miss a beat.

"Why and how do you know this?" Cherry asked.

"I don't know. I've just been looking up what people's names mean since I was a kid. Mine means only God can judge me. I like the idea of nominative determinism. It's like our parents seal our fate before we can even think."

"Okay. Do me next," Isaac requested.

"Also Hebrew, meaning you laugh a lot. Hey Cherry, what's your birth name?"

"This is my birth name. My parents were sort of hippies."

"Huh. I always thought it was a nickname," said Marcus. "Marissa, could I bother you for another cigarette?"

"Sure," she said, handing him one along with her Bic.

The misty rain stopped and the fog dissipated around the island. An almost full moon reflected the sun's light onto the obsidian sea. A cold southerly wind was rolling in but the group was sheltered by the hill that formed like a hand covering a lighter's flame.

"David said earlier that he ran into you with your man at the beach earlier," said Isaac.

"Yeah. We spent the morning swimming."

"They also said he's gorgeous," Marcus laughed. "How long have you two been together?"

"Like two and a half years now. We met at a bar where I was working. He was there for some corporate event. He came back the next night and asked me if I wanted to get coffee with him sometime."

"So of course you said yes," Danny said.

"Why wouldn't she?" Cherry asked, lighting another cigarette.

Isaac suggested they head down the hill and continue drinking in their suite. The room was warm when they returned and one of the bedroom doors was closed. Cherry took off her leather jacket and folded it on the kitchen counter. She grabbed a bottle of ouzo while Marcus grabbed five glasses. They all sat around the coffee table taking shots and discussing where they should go for their next holiday. It had been Vietnam the year before and Mexico the year before that. This year, Greece, and the next year they were thinking about Japan. In the middle of the discussion, Marcus closed his eyes and fell asleep leaning on the sofa arm. Once they'd shared the bottle and were all pleasantly drunk, they asked for Marissa's phone number so they could include her in their future plans, which she happily provided. Danny and Isaac excused themselves to the other bedroom which left Marissa and Cherry alone with Marcus sleeping silently on the couch. Cherry covered him with a blanket then asked Marissa if she wanted to go outside to smoke. They closed the door slowly and went downstairs.

"You know, when I was a kid, I didn't have a lot of friends. It was pretty much me and my brother. My parents got divorced when I was nine. I never saw my dad after that. I was pretty depressed in high school and just barely forced myself to get through uni. Then less than a month after I graduated, my mum had a heart attack at her office and she died. After her funeral I didn't know what to do so I just started traveling," Cherry said bluntly then lit a cigarette.

"I'm so sorry," Marissa said, not knowing how to comfort her. "I don't talk to my family much. We're not that close."

"When I met these guys last year it saved my life. They welcomed me as one of them and honestly I don't know what I would have done if I hadn't met them."

"They're really sweet."

"They're my family now. I mean, I still have my brother and we talk on the phone but these guys mean the world to me. I think sometimes a chosen family can be closer than a blood one."

"Yeah. That makes sense. Hey, I don't want to be too forward, but do you want to go back to your place for another drink? I'd invite you to mine, but..." Marissa asked.

"Sure," said Cherry.

The fog had cleared and from the top of the mountainous island the stars danced in the heavens. The moon, two days from being full, floated slowly across the sky. The bougainvillea's shadow on the wall opposite the window formed a dusky violet silhouette, steeped in the amber glow of the streetlamp, unmoving through the night. Cats prowled lazily through the narrow stone paths and buntings slept high in the cliffs and branches, fat and happy.

After putting her clothes back on and saying goodnight, Marissa stepped into the chilled air and lit a cigarette. The shadow bowed to hers as she passed under the streetlamp, then resumed its form. Sheltered from the wind by white houses, the silver smoke from the tip of her cigarette pirouetted into the darkness. She returned to the hotel a few hours before dawn and quietly slipped into bed.

CHAPTER ELEVEN

The *Dionisios Solomos* made port early the next morning at Karavostasis where Zack and Marissa were waiting, their backpacks slung across their shoulders. Marissa was relieved to discover the ferry had a spacious promenade deck. After boarding, they purchased two espressos from the boat's café and found two seats outside, facing the sea. On the bench beside them sat a deckhand, lazily sipping a cold coffee and puffing a cigarillo. A slight wind chopped the ocean surface but the day was warm and the sky was peppered with wispy clouds.

"It's just a little over an hour to Sikinos. I think you're really going to like it. It's not like Santorini or Mykonos or one of those party islands. I'm actually not quite sure what to expect but I know it will be peaceful. Nobody I've talked to has ever heard of it and I thought it would be nice to get away from civilization," Zack said. "I hope the hotel has a shaving kit."

"You didn't bring one?" Marissa lit a cigarette.

"No. I get nervous bringing a razor on a plane."

"I'm pretty sure you're allowed to."

"Still. Most hotels have them. And if they don't, there will probably be a pharmacy," Zack downed his espresso. "I think I'm gonna head back inside and grab a snack. You want anything?"

"I'm good. Thanks," Marissa exhaled a plume of smoke and

sipped her coffee slowly.

"You sure I can't tempt you with a cheese pie? You didn't have any breakfast."

"Yeah. I'm not really hungry. Maybe I'll just have a bite of whatever you get."

"Then I'm gonna grab something for you and if you don't want it now, you can just save it for later."

Marissa stared out across the stern. As Folegandros grew smaller in the distance, she saw the triangular peak jut out from the sea. The sunset from the monastery's courtyard was one she wouldn't forget for a long time. And the previous night's camaraderie just further down the slope - the nights she'd spent with Cherry... She was sad to be leaving Folegandros but also slightly relieved. She knew there would be no temptation on the next island. Nothing exciting. No thrill. No risk.

Zack returned with a piece of spanakopita and Marissa politely declined it. He left it on the table in front of her then announced he would sit inside where it was warmer. The roar of the diesel engine pushed the ferry further into the Aegean while Marissa scrolled through Instagram. She got up to throw away her empty cup and deposit her cigarette butt in the ashtray and, still scrolling, noticed Cherry's profile pop up as a person she may know. Instinctively and without second thought, she requested to follow her private profile. *Why hadn't we exchanged contact information sooner?*, she wondered. She lit another Marlboro Gold and saw from the corner of her eye the deckhand stand up to throw away his butt and get back to work.

A flock of yellow-legged gulls trailed the ferry as it moved between the islands. Looking up at them, Marissa remembered her childhood in San Diego. She used to wake up to their caws, as hundreds of them soared from the coastline to the neighborhood schools to forage for breakfast. When she was a child at the park, a seagull once swooped down and stole a sandwich directly out of her hands, sending her into a panicked crying fit. During one high school lunch, a seagull defecated on her friend's head and she laughed, explaining to her friend that it was good luck. The girl cried and went home early. Rats of the sky, her mother used to call them. Accompanied by her family on a day trip to Rosarito Beach, a group of red-eyed gulls with dirty feathers glared at them from the railing of a restaurant balcony while they ate lobster with beans and tortillas. The restaurant's owner, a friend of her grandmother, came to shoo away the birds with a broom but they simply returned to their perch after thirty seconds. Just like the cats on the islands, they'd beg and forage and do as their nature willed. An animal must act according to its nature.

The wind had strengthened by the time the ferry docked at Sikinos. In the center of the roundabout at the port was a massive Greek flag, fluttering in the gust. Zack and Marissa were the only people to depart. The boat pulled away without loading any new passengers less than a minute after their feet touched land. In the roundabout stood a heavyset bald man with a friendly black moustache and a large smile. He wore a navy blue wool sweater and khaki pants and leaned against a black Mercedes van and held a sign with the hotel's name on it.

"This is us," said Zack, guiding Marissa to the man.

"Kaliméra!" the mustachioed man said with a deep warm voice.

"Kaliméra," Marissa repeated.

"Come. Put your bags in the back. I take you to the hotel," he said, ushering them into the van.

Five minutes later, the van pulled into a communal dirt lot at the edge of a spattering of coastal houses.

"The road is too narrow ahead. You walk four minutes and the hotel is the one with the blue windows," he pointed across the water to the second farthest building by the sea. "I take your bags and meet you there."

He loaded their heavy backpacks into the trunk of a one seat electric car and zoomed ahead down the stone walking path. As Zack and Marissa walked through the village, they were met by an uneasy silence, as though the entire town was abandoned. There were no birds, no cats, no people, and no sounds or smells other than the salty spray of the crashing surf beside the path. In between the lifeless sun-bleached seaside homes were small alleys leading directly to the water. They reached the hotel in exactly four minutes, just as the man had told them. A lone olive tree stood in the courtyard, its leaves dulled by the autumn sun. The man smiled as he opened the door for them.

"Welcome. My name is Harry," he said, holding the door as they entered. He rushed behind the counter and fished out a set of keys from a basket. "You have already paid. Two nights. Please follow me. Your room is just this way," he led them to a door in the corner of a short hallway.

The door was unlocked and as Marissa stepped in, the first thing she noticed were the opened French doors leading to a small patio immediately overlooking the sea which, even in its slightly choppy state, held a translucent cyan color. Their room was on the second floor and the sound of waves and salty air made it seem as though they were staying on the beach. Behind a queen sized bed was a red brick wall and on the opposite wall was a small black desk.

"Help yourself to mini-fridge and please to call me if you have any questions. I live downstairs," Harry said. "Oh. There is only one restaurant open on the island. It is called Kapari. If you want, I can make you a reservation and drive you there tonight."

"I think we'll be okay," Zack said, noticing his backpack already placed on a folding luggage rack beside the desk.

"Okay. Well, let me know if you change your mind," he said, then left the room and gently closed the door behind him.

"Nice guy," said Marissa.

"Yeah. He seems cool."

They took turns showering then sat on the balcony and shared a cigarillo while watching the sea. The consistent breeze made the idea of swimming seem unappealing, so they decided to hike up the island's single mountain road to the central town to explore. Leaving the port town, they saw nobody in the village. When they crossed the promenade by the empty olive tree lined beach, they saw two old men sitting on old wooden ladder back chairs outside an unmanned café. They both looked vacantly across the cove before them, neither smoking nor drinking. Making their way up the hillside road, they saw a gas station next to a small market and they decided to stop inside. Zack picked up a block of feta cheese, a tomato, and two cucumbers, and Marissa grabbed a chocolate bar and a large bottle of water. Behind the counter was a short old woman with tied back white hair and a tawny complexion. Her eyes looked half closed. She didn't speak a word of English and wrote the amount of euros required for payment on a notepad. Marissa asked her for two packs of Marlboro Touch Blues then paid for their snacks.

A third of the way up the hill, Zack got tired and stopped to rest on a small boulder. He grabbed a cucumber from the plastic bag and crunched into it while Marissa opened a pack of Blues and lit one. Both tasted like nothing but served to refresh. While they rested, a car came down the hill and stopped next to them. A sturdy young man with a long brown beard and similarly long curly hair asked them if they needed a ride. Marissa told him "no thank you," and noticed wooden prayer beads hanging from his rear-view mirror. He reached into his central console and grabbed a business card, which he then handed to Marissa. He explained to her that he was the only taxi driver on the island and that if they needed a ride to call him. She thanked him and he continued downhill to the port.

After the brief rest, they continued up the street and turned onto an old walking path that ran further up the mountain that formed the island. It was as though they had stepped back in time. For the hour they walked up this path, they saw and heard nobody. Not even a braying donkey or a bird. The shrubs were brown and leafless and even the wind had decided not to follow them. They walked in silence, as though the sounds of their voices would disturb the serenity. The clicking of Marissa's lighter echoed through the hill as she lit another Blue, shamelessly discarding the old butt along the pristine path.

"You really shouldn't do that," Zack said softly.

"It's fine."

"It's so beautiful out here and you're really going to litter?"

"We do it all the time."

"It's different in a city. People are paid to clean the streets. But there's nobody here. It's fucked up to just make it somebody else's problem," he said, picking up the butt and putting it in the pocket of his jeans.

"It's really not a big deal Zack. Eventually the rain will take it to the sea."

"Then some turtle will eat it and he'll choke to death!"

"Like you give even half of a fuck about a turtle. You'd order one if it was on a menu. You're always going on about the shark fin soup you ate in San Francisco before they banned it," she said, not really knowing why she was being so argumentative.

"What's with you? All I'm saying is it's fucked up to litter in pristine wilderness."

"No matter where I throw it away, it'll end up in the ocean one way or another. The world's fucked and there's pretty much nothing we can do about it."

"Well not with that attitude."

They continued up the path.

"I don't have a fucking attitude. One person littering isn't going to save the world. And besides, if somebody cares, they will pick it up."

"That's me. I'm the guy that picked it up."

"Good for you."

"Are you just upset because you haven't eaten? Or is it that we didn't have sex today?"

Marissa laughed.

"I guess I'm just hungry. I'm sorry," she said, biting her tongue.

"Here. I still have that cheese pie from earlier," Zack pulled it from the plastic bag and handed it to her.

She put out her cigarette against the bottom of her shoe, set the butt on a small rock and stopped to eat the pie. Zack picked up the butt and tucked it in his pocket.

When they reached the island's central town, they found it eerily empty. There wasn't a single person on the stone paths and every house had its doors closed. Dozens of cats clustered on every street corner and eyed them as they walked past. Making their way further up the mountain town, passing white houses with blue window frames and short palm trees standing in each plaza, they started to smell the rich aroma of homemade stew wafting through the air. What few people there were on the island were grandmothers preparing traditional food alone in their kitchens while their families earned a living on the mainland, only coming to visit them in the summer. The cheese pie Marissa had eaten half an hour prior had satisfied her, but the smell of goat roasting in tomato and wine sauce made her stomach growl. More families of cats eyed them suspiciously as they pushed farther up the mountain, still not seeing a single person on the stone walkways. It was as though the island was under a spell and the people who lived there could only leave their homes when the sun wasn't out.

"Let's head up here," Zack suggested, pointing to a sign indicating a castle at the mountaintop.

Marissa took a sip of water and agreed, then followed him further up the mountain. There was no path, just an outcrop of gray boulders on a dusty hillside. On the top of the mountain, at the island's highest point, an ivory lime washed monastery overlooked the tranquil sea. They bowed their heads to enter the courtyard through a small archway and Zack walked around to take pictures. As Zack stepped up a very narrow staircase to survey the parapet and to photograph the sea and the village below the hill, Marissa noticed a gift shop. She stepped inside, again bowing through the low door and noticed an elderly nun knitting behind a low counter. In the shop were handmade candles, various bracelets and necklaces with wooden and cloth crosses, and a small shelf stocked with jars of honey made in the monastery. Wanting to make a donation, she bought a jar of honey and a small red cloth bracelet. The nun smiled and thanked her for the purchase. She returned to the courtyard and made her way to the chapel in the center. The inside was dark, lit only by lamps and candles. Effigies of saints painted in Greek orthodox style and surrounded by gold leaf covered every wall of the small room. Silence reigned inside this sacred place. Marissa could hear her heart beating and every breath she took sounded like wind on the sea. She lit a candle with a long wooden match, then stepped back into the sunlight.

Zack was still wandering along the parapet, crouching and closing one eye to capture well framed pictures, so Marissa walked the opposite direction to the side of the chapel that overlooked the sea. Folegandros stood on the horizon and she could make out, through the clear sky, the monastery that crowned it. She sat on a white stone staircase by the church's garden and lit a Touch Blue. The cerulean expanse looked calm from the mountaintop and she considered the ancient people of mythology using it as a roadway. *Odysseus would have been able to see every island as he sailed home from Troy. They're all so close to each other*, she thought. *How could he have drifted so far to the island of the Lotus-Eaters when it seems so easy to just hop from one island to another?*

"There you are," said Zack, turning the corner. "Oh wow. That's beautiful."

"Yeah it's a pretty great view."

"I meant you," he said, crouching to take a picture of her.

CHAPTER TWELVE

It was the middle of the afternoon when Marissa's phone chimed with a notification that Cherry had accepted the request to follow her. The sun was setting, enveloping the sky in a golden hue. Zack was swimming beside the hotel and Marissa was reading on the balcony. The narrator in her novel was traveling further north, getting gradually closer to the sheep he was searching for. As she read, the waves lapped against the concrete jetty below, forming a rhythmic lull. Zack's head bobbed up and down in the distant surf.

Marissa brought her book inside, placed it on the nightstand and grabbed her phone. Upon seeing the notification, she immediately smiled like a giddy child running to their mother outside of a school's gate. She unlocked her phone and scrolled through Cherry's profile, seeing all the places she'd documented, the foods she'd eaten, and the occasional selfie or picture of friends. Scrolling down more, she saw a photo of Cherry on a beach in Bali that somebody else had taken. In the photo, she wore a pink bikini and dark sunglasses while standing on an empty shoreline. The sky behind her was rosy pink and reflected off the still sea. Marissa set her phone down and started to touch herself. She moaned quietly and her pleasure was escalating when she heard some voices downstairs through the open patio door.

"How was it?" Harry asked, his voice muffled by the sea air.

"A little cold but not bad at all," Zack said, slightly short on breath.

"Good. Good. A little cold in October but you're young man. It's good for you. You sure you don't want me to make you dinner reservation?"

"What time does the restaurant open?"

"Seven o'clock. I save you a table."

"That would be great."

"I go around six thirty. You want to ride with me?"

"That's okay. I think we'll walk there."

"It's long walk."

"We did it earlier today. It wasn't so bad."

"As you like. I see you at seven."

Marissa heard Harry's thick hand as it fell on Zack's shoulder and patted appreciatively, as a shepherd does to his dog after a successful day. Her ecstasy eroded, she launched up from the bed, pulled her skirt back up, grabbed a cigarette, and returned to the patio. The sky was striated with rapidly darkening blood orange streaks when Zack walked into the room and toweled his hair dry.

"Hey Babe!" he almost yelled as he closed the door behind him.

"Hey," she replied weakly, her voice escaping her.

"You good for dinner at seven?" he asked, hanging up his towel on the shower curtain.

"Yeah. Sounds good," she coughed. The smoke from her Touch Blue drifted away on the breeze.

"I'm just gonna rinse off then we should head out," he stepped into the shower.

As the sun dipped lower in the amethyst sky, a thick mass of clouds, billowing and looming on the horizon, cast a pall over the majestic dusk. A few minutes later, amethyst turned to sapphire and Marissa heard the shower stop.

"Hey Babe, come inside," Zack beckoned.

"What's up?" she said, setting her pack of Marlboros on the desk.

"Do you think I could get a little blowjob before dinner?"

"Maybe later," Marissa sighed.

"You sure? Want me to go down on you first?"

"It's a little cold."

"We can close the door."

"Later Zack. I'm, like, really hungry. We've barely eaten today."

"Alright. I'll hold you to it. You good to walk there? It's another hour up the hill."

"Didn't the hotel guy offer to drive us?"

"Yeah, but I'd rather walk. You know, walking up these mountains is like the equivalent of a hundred flights of stairs? And it's beautiful out there. I bet the stars are gonna be crazy bright. There's, like, zero light pollution here,"

"Alright. Well, put some clothes on and let's get going then."

They experienced a few minutes of shimmering starlight before the storm rolled in. It came in a drizzle at first as they passed the line of olive trees by the shore. Marissa mentioned that they should have accepted Harry's offer to chauffer them there in his Mercedes and that launched Zack into a story.

"This is so fun though. It reminds me of when I was a kid and I hiked through the Grand Canyon with my dad. We were on this tiny path and I was riding a donkey while he led me on a rope. It started raining super heavily and then it got worse and started hailing. So my dad pulled me off the donkey and covered me with his jacket. We were like halfway up the path so we just had to deal with it. I started crying and my Dad told me everything was fine but I started screaming 'I don't want to die, I don't want to die,' and he started laughing. He slung me over his shoulder and the donkey followed us back up. The hail stopped after, like, ten minutes but the path was super muddy. You know, the Grand Canyon is so big that it creates its own weather system because of the difference in air pressure?"

"That's nice Zack. We're gonna be fucking drenched by the time we get up this mountain."

"The moral of my story is that you have to keep moving forward, even if it's hard. You're not gonna die. Just embrace the exhilarating. We're on an adventure. You're gonna remember this experience for the rest of your life."

"If we see that taxi driver, I'm flagging him down."

"Oh, come on... It's just forty more minutes."

The rain started falling straight down. Marissa managed to light a cigarette and held it down, facing the earth, in an effort to keep it dry.

"We've already walked up this mountain today, you know..." she said.

"Fine. If we see the cab, we take it. But I'm really close to thirty thousand steps. Babe. Turn around for a second."

Marissa turned her head to face the port. From a third of the way up the hill, a bright yellow light shone through the storm and illuminated the center of the horizon.

"That's Santorini," said Zack. "It's so crazy how we can see each island from the one next to it."

By the time they saw the taxi drive by, they had only five more minutes to walk before they got to the restaurant, so they continued on foot. Harry was waiting at the reception counter and his wife, a middle aged black haired woman with youthful black eyes and a friendly smile, stood polishing wine glasses behind the bar.

"Any table," Harry said, when Zack asked where they should sit.

They picked a table on the outdoor patio, shielded from the rain by a plastic awning. Four cats were sleeping under the chairs next to them. The black haired woman came to take their order and Zack asked for a carafe of white wine, oven grilled sardines, rusk and caper salad, and two orders of local lamb stewed in lemon sauce and a side of potatoes. She brought the wine two minutes later. Marissa enjoyed a dry cigarette as she downed her glass. Zack scrolled through his phone. When the sardines came a few moments later, the cats hurried to their table and put their front paws on Zack and Marissa's laps while looking up into their eyes. Zack flicked wine at them to urge them to go away, but their commitment was unwavering. Marissa gave a small orange cat a piece of fish. It consumed it instantly then begged for another.

"If you feed them, they won't stop begging," Zack warned.

"But they're just so adorable," she said, petting the cat on the back of its head.

Zack tried making noises at them to get them to go. Nothing seemed to work until Harry ran out with a spray bottle full of cold water and aggressively started shooting water at them and yelling in Greek. The cats ran outside but returned in a minute, sneaking in slowly, literally testing the water. By then, Zack had devoured the sardines and the cats had no interest in the caper salad.

"So. What do you think of this island so far?" Zack asked,

refilling their wine.

"It's peaceful. I like it," Marissa responded quietly.

"You okay?"

"Yeah. Just tired I guess. We walked a lot. And my clothes are still wet."

"Have more salad."

"It's a little salty."

"Well, yeah. It's just capers and olive oil. Of course it's salty. You don't like caperberries? They're fucking incredible. Have one."

"I'm good. You enjoy it."

"Want to order something else? You said you were starving."

"Yeah. Maybe. Do you remember what kind of pies they had on the menu?"

"I think just cheese pie," Zack said, enjoying a spoonful of oily capers and dry rusk.

"Can we get two?"

"I'm good. But I can order you one."

"I want two please. They're so good."

"Huh. So you liked the one from the boat earlier?"

"Yeah. So far I think that's been my favorite thing about the islands. The pies here are amazing. They're not really pies though. They're more like... turnovers."

"Well you know it's just a matter of translation. They call it pie here because of pita bread. Like spanakopita is just spinach plus pita. And in England they eat savory pies. I think it's just an American thing to bake sweet pies. Everything back home has way too much sugar."

"That makes sense."

"You know what would be good? A Greek style pie with cheese and apple," Zack said, stuffing another spoonful of capers into his mouth and breaking off a chunk of rusk.

Marissa sipped her wine and when the woman came to clear their dishes, she asked for two tiropitas and a second carafe of the same wine. The rain fell harder, slapping the plastic curtain next to their table. Zack asked Marissa for a cigarette and she handed him one along with her lighter. The cheese pies came out along with the spray bottle which, this time, did nothing to deter the cats. For them, it was either getting wet inside or getting soaked outside. Marissa ate one of the pies quickly and started slowly on the second.

"So I talked to Noah again today," said Zack.

"Oh yeah? How is he?" she sipped her wine and lit another cigarette.

"He's good. He said he's gonna try to make it work with Safa."

"That's good I guess. I mean, she really likes him. Did she even know he was thinking about ending things?"

"I don't think so, so please don't say anything to her. But he told me he'd thought about what I said - to not let politics get in the way of your sex life - and he agreed."

"Is it really all about sex with you guys?"

Zack laughed.

"Physical intimacy is important in a relationship," he said.

"Yeah. Sure. But so are shared values. How are they supposed to work if he's a zionist?"

"Who knows? Maybe someday there'll be some sort of peace there."

"You mean in the Middle East? Or in their relationship?"

96

"The Middle East."

"Yeah. Okay. And maybe someday I'll find out I had a long lost uncle who died and I'll inherit a couple million dollars."

"Heh. Maybe one day I'll win the lottery and we'll buy an island like this,"

"You already have," Marissa took a sip of wine and a drag from her Touch Blue.

"What do you mean?"

"Nothing."

"I don't get it. Are you saying I didn't earn what I have?"

"Please Zack. I didn't say that. I was kidding."

"I'm not a lottery winner. I'd fucking love to be. But I'm not."

"Okay. Sorry. It was just a joke."

After they'd each had three large glasses of wine, the lemon-sauced lamb was served to them and they both ate it ravenously, ignoring the begging cats. For dessert, they had local yogurt with honey from the monastery then Marissa insisted on paying the bill. Zack didn't let her. When their bill was settled, Harry insisted they wait out the storm and poured them each a shot of mastiha. They accepted it happily and sheltered for a few minutes, enjoying another cigarette at the table. During a lull in the downpour, they stepped outside and walked up the hill to the bus station. The night was dark and only one streetlamp stood by the station, glowing dimly. They inspected the bus schedule posted to a wooden board and saw that the last bus had stopped running hours ago and, as they didn't see a single bus all day, probably didn't even operate during the off season.

Faced with the misery of walking through pitch black rain,

Marissa fished out the taxi driver's business card from wallet and called him. Ten minutes, he said. She had no way of knowing, but her call had interrupted his dinner.

The taxi driver, Georgios, was a young man who lived with his grandmother in the central town. When he was five years old and during his first week of kindergarten, an earthquake struck the town of Ano Liosia, just north of Athens. He was playing in the schoolyard and didn't feel the tremor but he remembered the swinging power lines and the birds all flying upward at the same time. His mother was working in a hair salon at the time and the building collapsed on her. Rescue workers pulled her body from the rubble twenty hours later. She was five months pregnant when she died. His father was working construction and after the tragedy, he started drinking heavily. When Georgios was seven, he found his father hanging from the ceiling fan in the kitchen. He didn't know what to do so he sat sobbing on the floor for an hour before a neighbor heard and called the police. His grandmother took him in after that and he lived with her on Sikinos, earning a high school education then making a humble living seasonally harvesting olives and driving the taxi that used to belong to his grandfather.

"You called?" said Georgios from the driver's seat.

"Yeah. Thanks," Zack said, stepping into the back.

Marissa got in after him.

"Where to?" he asked the couple.

"Just down to the port is fine," said Marissa.

"Ten euro," he said.

98

"For a five minute drive?" Zack asked, annoyed.

"It's late. Price double for late night."

"Okay. Fine," Zack sighed.

The distant light of Santorini grew larger through the windshield as they moved downhill. The rain fell hard, and what would have been an hour-long walk on a cold stormy night was instead a five minute heated drive before a five minute stroll beside an angry sea. When they got out, Zack handed Georgios exactly ten euros and thanked him. On their walk back, the rain started falling harder.

They were both still tipsy when they returned to the room. Marissa switched on the light and Zack embraced her, planting a kiss on her lips. She kissed him back and they were on the bed a minute later. She felt his erection under his pants, and having not gotten relief earlier that afternoon, peeled them off. He grabbed the back of her head with measured force and, taking his meaning, she treated him to a blowjob before drunkenly throwing her clothes off and straddling him. It was the first good sex they had since Athens.

Zack fell asleep within minutes of finishing, not even getting up to brush his teeth. Marissa used the restroom then put on a pair of sweatpants and a pull-over hoodie and stood outside next to the wet chairs. She lit a cigarette and unlocked her phone, opening Instagram immediately. Zack had posted a picture of the sardines they'd eaten for dinner. There were some posts about animal shelters in New York offering special deals, waiving adoption fees due to overcrowding. She clicked through various stories and advertisements before seeing Cherry's. It was a picture of an orange buoy affixed to a ferry's gunwale. In the background was the luminous blue sea below the same brushed coral sunset she'd seen earlier. The platinum colored smoke from her neglected cigarette dawdled upward, langouring in the windless night's humidity.

CHAPTER THIRTEEN

They woke up late the next morning. For breakfast, they shared the block of feta and the tomato on the balcony. Zack went inside to make coffee and grab the chocolate bar and Marissa lit her morning cigarette. The night's storm had passed and the day was sunny and clear. There were no birds in the sky, no people at the beach or the port and, from the balcony, the only sound was the gentle lapping of the sea against the jetty below.

"So, what's the plan for today?" Zack asked, returning with coffee in hand.

"I don't know. Whatever you wanna do," she said, taking her cup from him so he could sit comfortably.

"Well, there's this winery at the other side of the island but it's almost a two hour walk and I'm pretty sure it's closed for the season. There's lowkey nothing to do here except swim and fuck. We've already explored the only town and seen the view from the church. I guess we could walk to another beach just over the hill and spend the day there. Maybe grab more things from the market for a picnic?"

"Sounds good. Let me just finish my coffee and take a shower and we can get ready to go."

"No rush. Take your time. I have to check in with the office so I'm going to make a quick call while you shower," Zack said, opening

OFF SEASON

the chocolate bar and breaking off a piece.

Marissa lit another cigarette and waited for her coffee to cool so she wouldn't burn her tongue.

"Last night was fun," Zack said.

"Yeah," Marissa agreed.

"You know, this is so incredible. Just being in the islands with you. I had no idea what to expect on this trip but the food is all so amazing and, like, all these towns are so rustic and charming and it's just so cool to be able to share it with someone. When I went to Singapore a few years ago, it was just me. I mean, I stayed at Marina Bay Sands and had a great time but, it's like, I show people pictures and my story highlights on instagram and it feels like a dream instead of real life. But, being here with you now, it's like there's this foundation of reality. Like, proof that we're actually here. You know what I mean?"

"Totally. Solo travel is nice too though. I think social media has sort of ruined us in the sense that our vacations need to be validated. Like, it's not enough to explore or see a new place. We feel this need to share it with everybody," Marissa took a drag of her Touch Blue.

"Well maybe. But I'm not so sure about that. Back in the nineties, people used to gather their friends and family and show them photo albums or slideshows. It's just human nature to want to share joy with the people we care about. Social media just makes it easier, more immediate."

"You don't think there's a level of braggadocio to it? Like, I feel like people are always in soft competition with each other to see who can spend more or see a prettier sunset, or like, who looks best in a bikini."

102

"I guess. But that's not why I post shit," Zack said, the caffeine lying on his behalf. "I just want to show people that I'm having a good time."

"You posted a story yesterday of your watch. How is that not bragging?"

"I appreciate the craftsmanship. You know there's thirty five rubies in this thing's movement?"

"See. That right there is bragging."

"If you see it that way..." Zack said. "If you view life as a competition, you'll never be happy. My colleagues take their two weeks on chartered yachts with private chefs. Noah flew to Vegas and Miami last year on a private jet."

"His family's rich."

"My family has some money too, but I don't think any of us are rich. It's crazy how people live. We had this client that we took out to Daniel for a dinner. He ordered a bottle of La Tache that cost like fifteen grand. The food wasn't even that good. But they did press this duck tableside, like, crushing the whole thing into a sauce... I think there are diminishing returns when it comes to wealth and lifestyle. Like, look at these billionaires eating at mid-tier restaurants. In practice, what's the difference between a billion and fifty million?"

"I'm going to take a shower," Marissa said, putting out her cigarette.

"It's just a bigger yacht," Zack was talking to himself.

Feeling energetic and restless, Zack looked at porn on his phone while Marissa showered. He picked up his book from the nightstand when he heard the water stop. She stepped out of the steamed restroom in a robe and rummaged through her backpack for her brown bikini. As she tossed the robe on the chair and stepped into her swimsuit, Zack set his open book on his lap.

"Very nice. How much?" he said in his Borat voice.

"Come on Zack. You should get ready," she turned away from him while putting on her top.

"Give me a smile Baby. Why angry face?" he continued.

She turned to him with her hands on her hips and an annoyed grin.

"Wawaweewa!"

"Get ready," she commanded, stifling a laugh.

Zack stood from the bed and stepped onto the balcony to grab his swimsuit from the line where it was drying. It was still cold and wet from the night's rain.

"I like you. I like sex," Zack said, still affecting Borat while packing things into the beach bag.

They stopped at the market up the hill from the port and bought everything they'd need for a greek salad, plus some bread and two cans of sardines. They also made sure to get two large water bottles before their trek over the hill to the beach. As they descended the dirt path, the turquoise water in the distance reflected sunlight like diamond dust. When they got there, there was nobody. A small grove of olive trees stood behind a line of rocks that separated the hard earth from the beige sand. Marissa set out their towels and Zack stripped naked and ran into the clear water.

The narrator of her Murakami book had made it to the pasture where the sheep was and had fallen asleep only to wake up to his girlfriend having disappeared. The cold imagery and dreamlike darkness existed in stark contrast to Marissa's surroundings, but somehow the feeling of isolation, agnosia and inchoateness spoke to her soul. She put the book down and took a sip of water. Zack's head bobbed in the distance like a seabird. She thought about her apartment back home, that little hovel on East Fourth Street, no bigger than the hotel rooms they'd stayed in. The moldy staircase up to the third floor and the sounds of their neighbors fighting and having sex. And the stomping on the floor from above... She missed the dogs she walked around Tompkins Square Park but as she sunbathed on the deserted beach on that empty island, she felt like it wouldn't matter if she ever went home - as though she had nothing to lose.

"Fuck!" Zack yelled, his voice carrying over the flat water.

Marissa sat up.

Zack emerged from the sea, staggering like he was drunk.

"Fuck! I think I just got bit by a fish," he said, collapsing on his towel. He angled his leg, twisting his ankle to expose his foot. It was bleeding at the side. Marissa poured some water on the wound.

"Does it hurt?" she asked.

"It stings like a bitch," he said, wrinkling his nose in pain.

"You'll be okay. It's probably not poisonous. Just rest."

"Fuck. It hurts. It's turning blue!"

"That's just your body healing."

"Can you look up what bit me? What if it's poisonous?"

"Did you see it?"

"No, but I put my foot down on the sand for a second and felt a sharp sting."

Marissa checked her phone to find the fish that could have bit him and found an article saying that a fisherman in Crete had caught a silver-cheeked toadfish that had enough venom to kill thirty men. Another possible culprit was the weeverfish, who's neurotoxin stung worse than a wasp but was not lethal.

"I think it could be a weeverfish," she said. "They hide in the sand and it says here their spines contain a poison that isn't lethal to humans."

"Little cocksucking bastard! Fuck!"

"Just try to relax. You'll be fine."

"God damn it hurts. You were right. We should have just gone to Paris. This fucking island is cursed."

Marissa tried not to laugh. She lit a cigarette for him and put it in his mouth, as if he was a soldier who'd just taken a bullet on a battlefield. Zack fell asleep on his towel after the pain subsided fifteen minutes later. The beach was still empty and the sun was still bright. Marissa sat, draped in a sarong with her bikini underneath, and scrolled through Instagram, stopping occasionally to check Zack's pulse. She saw that Cherry had posted a picture of the blue domed rooftops in Santorini.

A gentle breeze rolled in and Zack woke to the chilled air on his bare skin. He said he was still in pain and asked for Marissa to prepare him a salad. They had no plates or bowls so she just handed him ingredients to take one bite at a time. He drank more water and perked up.

"Babe. I think I need you to suck the venom out. It still hurts. I'm going to die here."

"You're literally fine."

She put her hand over his forehead. It felt normal.

"I think the venom's made its way to my dick. It's starting to get blue and stiff. I need you to suck it out."

"Yeah. You're fine,"

"You're just going to let me die? On vacation? I see how it is. My tombstone is gonna read 'Here lies Zackary Wilson, deceased in his twenty sixth year, whose unloving girlfriend refused to suck the venom from his wound.'"

"If it will make you shut up," she laughed.

She grabbed a hair tie from the beach bag and tied her hair into a ponytail. He tasted like salt water. He became fully erect then asked her to take her bikini off. She refused, saying she didn't want to risk an infection.

After satisfying him, Marissa continued reading and Zack sent an email to the hotel in Santorini then purchased new ferry tickets online so they could leave Sikinos early to escape the curse. The original plan was to spend two nights there, but he felt that he'd seen enough and it would be too difficult to walk up the mountain road with his wounded foot. He grabbed his James Bond book and read next to Marissa for an hour and a half until they both finished their novels. They each smoked a cigarette then opened their tinned sardines and ate them by hand before washing the oil off in the ocean.

Zack's body ached tremendously as he walked back over the hill. He was fully sunburnt and throbbing pain lingered and pulsated with every step. Mostly though, he was upset that Marissa had refused to disrobe on the beach. He desperately wanted to take pictures of her first wearing her swimsuit then wearing only sunglasses so he could masturbate to them later. However, he never vocalized this request for fear of angering her. If he would have asked, she would have obliged him but his uncharacteristic timidity in this specific want overrode his lust. He'd never spoken to her about his swimsuit fetish. And as they walked down the hill back towards the port, he realized that he had never asked about her fantasies.

"Babe. Tell me. What's your biggest sexual fantasy?" he asked, needing to distract himself from the pain.

"That's random. What's yours?"

She walked behind him, holding the beach bag.

"I asked first."

"I don't know. I don't really have any."

"That's such bullshit. Everybody has one. Come on. You can tell me."

"Really. I don't know."

"You can't think of anything that seems fun?"

"What do you want me to say?"

"I don't know... I won't judge you."

"I don't really have a fantasy, but I guess being blindfolded sounds fun," she said.

"Really?"

"Well, you asked! Now what's yours?"

"I think it would be so sexy to take nude pics of you in public."

"No way."

"No. I mean like on the beach just now. With nobody around."

"Well if there's nobody else there then I guess that would be okay."

"Yeah?"

"Maybe. I don't know."

The conversation worked to distract Zack from the stinging.

When they returned to the hotel, he ran his foot under hot water until it felt better, then joined Marissa on the balcony for a cigarette. She declared that she was going to take a shower and Zack asked her if he could take those pictures he wanted while she stood on the balcony. Feeling sorry for him, she agreed to it.

CHAPTER FOURTEEN

Above the scarlet horizon sat the last gold of the day, rapidly thinning, while the unclouded sky glowed emerald green at the foot of the heavens. The colors refused to meet. The evening was unusually warm and a dry wind swept across the sea, propelled by the coming night. The Greek flag fluttered in the port's roundabout as the *Dionisios Solomos* put in. Zack and Marissa stood waiting with their full backpacks slung over their shoulders. Marissa returned to the same seat on the upper deck that she'd sat in the day before and Zack joined her for a cigarette. As the ferry moved further into the sea, the sky darkened and the full moon reflected white light across the ocean's surface. Zack went inside to take a nap and Marissa stayed out, chain smoking and scrolling through Instagram. The same deckhand took a seat at the table beside her and slowly sipped coffee while sending text messages. Turning towards him briefly, she felt a *déjà vu*. She wondered how long it had been since her vacation to Greece had begun, then took a moment to count the days. Two nights in Athens, two in Milos, two in Folegandros, one in Sikinos. Only a week. The time had passed like flowing molasses. She was starting to forget the rhythm of the city; maybe even starting to forget the harmony of the life she'd made for herself back home.

As the ferry rounded the caldera, Marissa finished the last of her

Touch Blues. The boat's loudspeaker chimed on and announced in Greek that in a few minutes they would make port in Thíra. Marissa stepped inside and found Zack asleep and drooling. She nudged him awake.

They disembarked with the rest of the tourists. A uniformed man stood beside a bulky black van, holding a sign reading *Mr. Wilson* and the hotel's name. The man took their backpacks and they settled into their seats. Marissa started feeling physically unwell as the van twisted its way up the steep hill leading from the port to the island's ridge. Ten minutes later they arrived at a small white arch by the side of the road. A young woman stood behind a black lectern, waiting for them. She had black hair tied back in a ponytail and wore thick rimmed glasses and a tight fitting black pantsuit with a white silk blouse underneath. Her makeup was applied tastefully and she had deep brown eyes and long eyelashes, thick with mascara.

"Hello Mr. and Mrs. Wilson," she said as a bellhop appeared and offered to take their backpacks. "Welcome to the Petit Palace Suites. If you'll please follow me, I'll show you to the bar and give you a brief introduction to the island and the hotel."

Marissa felt lightheaded and hungry as they walked down a small flight of stairs to the bar. The spectacled woman pulled out a chair for her at a table overlooking the caldera and another hotel employee brought them two glasses of mint lemonade. Marissa took a sip and wished it had gin in it.

"Did you have a pleasant journey on the ferry today?" the hostess asked.

"Yeah. We just came from Sikinos," said Zack.

"Oh. That's quite different from here. Very rustic. Not many

111

tourists go there. What did you think of it?"

"It was really peaceful. Really quiet," said Zack, smiling and maintaining strong eye contact with the hostess.

"That's good to hear. Let me tell you a little about the island before I show you to your room," she pulled a folding map from a small blue folder and set it on the table. Then she grabbed a matching blue pen from her breast pocket and clicked it. "So we are here," she said, circling the hotel's location. "Just north of us is the town of Fira. You will find good restaurants there and many small shops. There are nightclubs too if that interests you. The hotel has a bus that comes every hour, from noon until eight, and will take you straight there. There's no charge for that. It leaves on the hour and returns here fifteen minutes later from the same place it drops you off. From Fira, there is a hiking trail that leads to the town of Oia and boasts a spectacular view of the caldera. Oia is a beautiful town but I recommend you visit there early in the morning before it becomes too crowded. The best way to see the island is by car. A taxi to Oia can cost up to forty euros and to rent a car for the day is forty five so we highly recommend you rent one if you want to explore the different towns. There is a rental office less than five minutes from the hotel. To the south is Megalohori, which has many buildings with traditional architecture. If you visit there, you can see the island the way it was many years ago. There are beaches on the northern side and southern side of the island. Both are very beautiful. And finally, there are the ruins of the Ancient Thíra and Akrotiri, if you are interested in history. Over three and a half thousand years ago, the volcano erupted here, creating the caldera. The ruins of the old cities are largely intact and show life as it was back then."

"That sounds pretty cool. I'd love to check that out," said Zack, still unwaveringly focused on the hostess.

Marissa was uninterested in the spiel and was staring at the full moon's reflection on the still sea which, from the side of the cliff, looked stable and motionless.

"Do you have any questions about the island?" the hostess asked.

"No. I think we're good," Zack said.

"Great. Breakfast is included with your room and is served here at the bar restaurant from seven to ten thirty. You may order anything from the menu. The pool is open until seven at night and feel free to ask for extra towels. This is the bar, open from noon until eleven. You may order drinks poolside as well. There is room service available at all hours. As well, we offer catamaran tours of the island. They leave in the early afternoon and take you to the caldera. There is a chef on board and dinner is served on the boat at sunset. It's usually grilled meat and fish. We would be happy to arrange that for you if you are interested. Do you have anything special planned for your stay here in Santorini?"

"We have a reservation at Perivolas tomorrow night," Zack said.

"That's an excellent restaurant. Great choice," said the hostess. "If you're ready, I can lead you to your room."

"Sure," Zack said, beaming as he stood.

Marissa finished what was left of her lemonade then chugged Zack's before following them. The hostess led them to an elevator, pressed a button for them to go down and stepped out. A minute later, the elevator opened to a large tunnel and at the end of it, the hostess stood waiting for them. *How did she get there so fast?* Marissa wondered.

"Right this way to your room," she ushered them across a narrow white path and led them to a large suite with a panoramic view of the sea and the caldera - the same view as the bar's. Outside the French door that opened to their room was a private hot tub and a wooden table with two cushioned chairs. Everything was bleach white. Inside the room was a king sized bed, a small blue couch against the wall facing a coffee table and a console with a remote that controlled the curtains, a complimentary bottle of white wine and a room service menu. Their backpacks were already on the folding luggage rack waiting for them.

"Is there anything else I can help you with this evening, Mr. Wilson?" the hostess asked.

"I think we're all set. Thank you so much," he said, eager to settle in.

"Excellent. Enjoy your stay," she smiled then left.

Marissa went straight to the restroom and Zack opened the menu to see what was available. When she got out, Zack opened the bottle of wine and poured two glasses. Marissa changed into sweatpants and a hoodie that were still dirty from their time in Athens then they sat outside to drink and smoke. All they had left was a pack of Delph cigarillos Zack had purchased by the beach in Folegandros. They were strong compared to the Touch Blues and the combination of the pure tobacco and the wine made her more lightheaded.

"What do you think of the wine? It's assyrtiko. Produced locally," said Zack.

"Not bad. I wish it was chilled though."

"That would be nice... Should we get in the hot tub?"

"I think I should eat something first. I'm dying."

"That's probably a good idea. Let's just order room service. Then tomorrow, we can rent a car and explore the island."

"You said we had a reservation tomorrow?"

"Yeah. I made it on the ferry before I passed out. It looks like the best restaurant in Santorini. I also found a place for lunch tomorrow that seems good. But it's on the other side of the island..."

"I'm down for whatever you want to do."

"Want to look at the menu before I order dinner?"

"You can just pick something for me," Marissa said, puffing the cigarillo. It burned slowly. The wine was bone dry and slightly citrusy. It had a saline aftertaste that reminded her of the afternoon on the empty beach.

"Everybody on the islands is so nice. It's crazy. We haven't met a single rude person the entire time we've been here," Zack said, returning to the table. "Like, back in New York, everybody has their guard up. People are nice there too but you have to, like, earn their respect first. It's like, there's no stress here. Just pure vibes. What would you think about living here some day?"

"In Santorini? I don't know. We just got here."

"Just the islands in general. Imagine our retirement. I buy a thirty-footer and we just sail around and live on a boat. We stop in towns to get things for salad and pasta sauces and..."

"You know I get seasick."

"Oh. Yeah. Well it's just an idea," Zack sipped his wine.

Their dinner arrived half an hour later. A greek salad, two plates of lamb chops with roasted vegetables and a wine sauce, and two slices of chocolate cake along with another bottle of the same local wine. They ate at the table outside, finishing their meal quickly but taking their time with dessert. The cake was rich and moist and under the full moonlight, unobscured by clouds, the wine in their glasses sparkled. The heavy smoke rising slowly from the tip of the Delph shone silver in the night.

"Babe. I have an idea. And feel free to say no," Zack said, pouring more wine.

"What's that?" Marissa asked.

"Let's make a sex tape. In the hot tub."

He had a full bottle of wine in him. Marissa sighed, took a long puff and exhaled slowly. She lowered her eyelids, as if to say no without words.

"Yeah - No," she said firmly. Remembering the mirror in Athens, the idea actually intrigued her but she was exhausted. She didn't even feel like having sex with him, let alone being filmed in the act.

"You sure? It would be so fun..."

"You know what? Fuck it. Let's do it. But let's finish this bottle," she snuffed out the Delph in the ashtray.

"Really!?"

"If it makes you happy."

"Well only if it's something you want to do," he sipped his wine, eager to finish it.

"I already said sure."

"God, I love you," Zack said. He stood up, walked over to her chair, gently rubbed the underside of her chin to tilt her head up and kissed her.

When the bottle was empty, Zack went inside to grab his phone and threw off his clothes. He came back out smiling and eased into the hot tub. Marissa's head was spinning when she got up from her seat, but she took off her clothes and joined him in the warm water. Without giving her a moment to acclimate to the water, he kissed her neck and caressed her thigh. It felt nice, but both the heat of the tub and her nerves were increasing her heart rate. She took a deep breath, then said "wait," and hoisted herself up to sit on the tile rim.

"You good Babe?" he asked.

"Just really lightheaded. I need a moment."

Zack moved across the square tub to get a better view of his girlfriend in the moonlight, the steam rising from her body as beads of water and sweat trickled down her bare breasts, slowly finding their way to her hips.

"Fuck. You're so beautiful," he said, ignoring his own rising blood pressure.

Marissa tilted her head up and breathed slowly. She felt a soft breeze coming up from the sea. *How much did I smoke?* Marissa thought, feeling almost deliriously lightheaded. The switch from the light Marlboros to the pure slow smoking Delphs hit her as though she'd had an entire cigar. And she essentially had. She was starting to feel dizzy and she carefully got out of the tub.

"I think I need to lie down," she said.

"Have some water."

Zack followed her inside and grabbed a bottle of Acqua Panna from the mini fridge. He poured some into a glass and handed it to her. She sat up to grab it and took a small sip.

"You okay?" he asked her, taking the glass from her and setting it on the nightstand.

"Not really," she replied.

He helped her under the blankets and she closed her eyes. He switched off the lights then sat next to her for a few minutes until she fell asleep. Her breath whispered softly through the room's silence, forming a melodic cadence. Zack returned to the hot tub and scrolled through the pictures he took earlier that afternoon, silently lamenting his decision to order the second bottle.

Chapter 15

"You look like a lobster," Marissa said, sipping a cappuccino. Harsh sunlight poured through the bar's panoramic window. A waiter came with a feta omelet and a fruit salad. Zack had already eaten half of his eggs benedict.

"Yeah. I got fucked up yesterday. At least my foot feels better. I always get a sunburn on vacation. It's God's way of punishing me for being white. But I read somewhere that if I eat tomatoes and dark chocolate, it will help me heal faster."

"Really? That works?"

"I think so. Today it will hurt and tomorrow it should start itching. I got a second degree sunburn in Cancun when I was a kid, so this is nothing."

It was still early, and Marissa walked back downstairs to the room to shower while Zack rented a car. After toweling herself dry and applying makeup, she put on a pair of white linen pants, a yellow shirt and her denim jacket then made herself an espresso in the room. She took it to the outdoor table to enjoy it with the view. A cruise ship sat motionless in the center of the water between the island and the caldera, and scores of smaller vessels cruised around it like remoras beside a shark. She finished her coffee and went upstairs to wait for Zack. He'd been in a rush earlier and she didn't want to keep him waiting.

He pulled up to the white roadside arch in a Polaris off-road vehicle - something resembling a beach buggy but with sharper lines.

"You couldn't find a normal car?" she asked, stepping into the passenger side.

"This was all they had left. Sixty euros a day too. I got you a little something from the shop next door," he said, handing her a plastic bag. Inside were two packs of Marlboro Gold, a large bag of tzatziki flavored Lays, a dark chocolate bar, and a white baseball cap with 'Santorini' embroidered in blue.

"You're a lifesaver," she said, immediately ripping open a pack and lighting a cigarette. She put on the cap to protect her hair from the wind. Zack stepped on the accelerator and the Polaris sprung into action, instantly getting to speed and flying up the road.

"The torque on this thing is crazy," he yelled over the engine.

"Can you slow down?" she asked, the wind eating away at her cigarette.

"Not really," he yelled. "It seems faster than it is. We'll be there soon."

Marissa held on to the car's metal railings during the twenty five minute journey to Oia. Zack was driving as though he was being pursued, enjoying every chicane. There had been other, more modest options at the car rental desk, but Zack didn't want to avoid the inevitable argument that would occur if Marissa had tried playing the new Taylor Swift album. He wanted today to be perfect.

"Jesus Zack! Did you not hear me telling you to slow down?" Marissa asked, stepping out of the car in the communal dirt lot beside the town.

"Sorry Babe. Couldn't hear you over the engine. We were just going the speed of other cars. It just felt faster cuz it has a smaller wheelbase."

"Could you maybe just drive a little slower next time? I don't care if we hold up traffic. It's no fun for me if I feel like we're about to go off the road."

"Okay. Sorry. We're not going to go off the road but I'll try," he said.

They left the bag of snacks in the car and started in the direction of the town. It was about midmorning when they got to the center of Oia. The flagstone path running through the ridge of the town was freshly washed. On both sides stood small white-walled shops selling gold jewelry and souvenirs. A lone pygmy palm tree stood outside an unopened restaurant and bougainvilleas clung to the rooftops of every third building.

Following the map on Zack's phone, they turned down a narrow alley and saw a queue of tourists speaking Spanish. They were waiting to take an unobstructed picture in front of the three blue domes. The landmark's signature hue off-set the sun bleached buildings, majestic and unbothered by the light, as if it were enamel, mirroring the sea in the distance. Marissa wanted to keep exploring the narrow paths but Zack insisted they wait in line to take a photo together. *What's the point of a picture that everybody else has?* Marissa thought. But the line moved quickly and when it was their turn, Zack handed his phone to the people behind them and asked if they would take a photo. They happily agreed and, after a few seconds, Zack thanked them and scrolled through the pictures. The sun was behind them in the photos and they were slightly silhouetted. The domes looked dull in the unadjusted lighting and the composition was executed without thought. He tried editing the photo on his phone while Marissa smoked another Gold.

"Let's keep going," Zack said, holding Marissa's hand as they walked through the maze of narrow staircases that characterized the town. Every building around them was a hotel, and they passed youthful uniformed employees hoisting full suitcases on their shoulders and moving quickly through the growing throng of tourists. Zack silently admired their strength. They both stopped frequently at various points to take pictures before reaching a castle at the edge of town. They followed the path to the top of the turret. A man sat on a wooden chair, playing medieval tunes on a lute with a hat resting at his foot to collect donations. The view was panoramic. The sun had ascended considerably in the sky, its light's intensity yielding to the passing day.

Zack turned to take a picture of the hillside town, then they agreed that Oia was underwhelming unless you happened to be staying there and they made their way back to the Polaris.

"Remember, slowly please this time," Marissa said in the parking lot.

"Sure thing," he said.

He was gentle on the gas as they continued their loop of the island. After fifteen minutes of driving along the northern coast to the sound of a roaring engine, he pulled the vehicle over on the side of the road and got out to survey a beach. There were small pebbles lining the shore where sand should be and piles of rotting kelp stretched as far as he could see.

"This doesn't look so great," Zack said.

"We can go somewhere else. I don't mind," Marissa agreed.

So they stepped back into the Polaris and continued around the island. The tan foliage looked dead around them. There were more gas stations by the roadside than animals. They drove past resort hotels and abandoned buildings and the whole place felt very unnatural, as though it never recovered from the eruption three thousand years ago. At a fork in the road, Zack asked Marissa if she wanted to have an early lunch and she liked the idea, so they turned toward the heart of the island to get to the southern shore, about twenty five minutes away.

They parked behind a restaurant called To Psaraki, which Zack had carefully selected. Outside, across the road from the restaurant, was an array of tables covered in blue gingham cloth that overlooked a small harbor filled with fishing boats. A waiter showed them to one of the tables, and brought them a bottle of water and two menus.

"This place has probably the best fish on the island," Zack said, folding his menu shut after quickly deciding what to order. "Want me to just order for us?"

"Sounds good," she said. She lit another cigarette and offered one to Zack. He declined, saying he'd prefer to wait until after the meal.

When the waiter came, Zack ordered fried sardines, grilled octopus, roasted vegetables with a red snapper grilled whole, and a bottle of white wine. The waiter, a young local man, said "Thank you," in between each of Zack's requests. Marissa found it endearing. A small flock of gulls circled the air above the moored vessels as the waiter brought the wine alone with bread and olive oil. Marissa drank slowly, not wanting to relive the previous night. Zack's full body burn was starting to ache, so he almost chugged his first glass of wine and asked Marissa for a cigarette. He drank half a glass of water, then lit his

Marlboro Gold.

"So. What's the plan for today?" Marissa asked.

"There's a beach right down the hill from us. I thought we could relax there for a few hours, then maybe head to the hotel for a nap before dinner. Unless you wanted to see those ancient ruins."

"No. A nap sounds nice. We've been moving non-stop."

"And we have the hot tub too. I feel like the only thing to do here is eat and make love," Zack realized verbally.

Marissa chuckled and sipped her wine.

"Isn't that what you said about the other island?" she asked.

He gazed up, trying to remember.

The waiter came with the sardines and the octopus at the same time and they ate them slowly, enjoying the scenery. The food was prepared simply but tasted very fresh.

"So Babe, I was thinking, and it's just a thought, but I feel like maybe we're ready to move into a bigger place."

"Yeah?"

"I've been saving a lot of money and my cousin, Mike, is going to move to Hoboken in a couple of months with his wife. He offered us his apartment in Chelsea for five thousand a month. And honestly, that's a steal."

"That still seems like a lot more than we're paying now."

"I know. But I think we can afford it and it would be so great to have more space. Your business is doing well and like I said, I'm saving a lot, so I think we deserve an upgrade. And I think if we do this, we should make a decision soon because he could probably rent it for six or six five. We'd be getting the family rate."

"I mean, if we're each paying twenty five hundred, that's thirty grand a year. That's a huge step up from what we're paying now. I mean... It's like double."

"I just think this is the logical next step in our relationship. We can't stay in a studio forever. And we're not going to find another opportunity like this. I don't want to move to fucking Williamsburg or Bedford, and I do think we need more space. Not from each other, but in general. You know, like, to hold clothes and stuff."

Marissa finished the octopus on her plate and lit another cigarette.

"We can talk about it more later. Just thought I'd let you know because I really want to jump on this," Zack said, pouring himself more wine.

"It *would* be nice to have a bigger place." Marissa contemplated out loud.

"Right? And it's Chelsea! We'd be getting an almost two thousand a month discount. It's a no brainer."

"I guess it's a good idea."

"I'm going to text him right now. He's probably just waking up."

"Can I have a little more time to think about it? Like, there may be cheaper options."

"Sure. But I'd like to get back to him soon. So maybe I'll just text him now and ask him if he can give us a few days to think about it."

"It *does* sound like a decent idea though."

The waiter came to clear their plates and in the harbor below, a group of tourists loaded out of a bus and onto a catamaran.

"I love you so much, Marissa," Zack said. "I'm serious. This is probably one of the best vacations of my life and I'm so stoked to be sharing it with you."

"You're sweet. I love you too," she replied, unable to tell if his cheeks were red from the sun, the alcohol, or both.

The snapper arrived at the table on a massive porcelain platter and the waiter apportioned it onto a serving dish. The meat was succulent and the skin was salted well. There was no sauce, but the roasted vegetables balanced the flavor nicely. While they ate the fish, Zack asked Marissa about her work but she didn't have much to report. She picked up the dogs, she took them to the park, she took pictures of them for their owners, she cleaned up after them, then brought them back to their respective apartments. It was a decent gig.

When the waiter came back, Zack asked for two orders of galaktoboureko to which he replied "Thank you," before clearing the plates.

"If we move into a bigger place, what would you think about us adopting a dog?" Marissa asked.

"*When* we move into a bigger place, you can adopt as many dogs as you want Babe. Just as long as I don't have to pick up their shit."

"You wouldn't help me take care of it?" she asked, half jokingly.

"I mean, you know. I'd just rather not clean up after one. I don't mind if you want one but the thought of cleaning another creature's shit disgusts me."

"What about a baby?"

"You want a kid?"

"No. I mean like, what about changing a diaper? Just hypothetically."

"Well. That's different. That's, like, life we created. You just have to. It's non-negotiable. But a dog? No. That's subservience."

"You know that's what I do for a living, right?"

"You're getting paid. I handle shit at work too. That's what all work is - dealing with shit. There's a word for people who don't handle shit all day. Unemployed. I'd just rather not do it off the clock. Like, when I'm chilling at home or it's the weekend, the last thing I want to do is scoop up warm dog shit and carry it around," he tried to pour more wine but the bottle was empty.

The waiter came with the dessert and Zack consumed his in three frenzied bites. Marissa found it too sweet and the spiel had eliminated her appetite so she let Zack eat it. She offered to pay but he wouldn't let her. Once the bill was settled, they were both too drunk to drive so they left the Polaris parked behind the restaurant and sauntered down the hill for about ten minutes in the direction of the water.

Arriving at the beach, they saw rows of loungers shaded by straw thatched umbrellas. At the foot of a tall chalky cliff stood a bar, and a small wooden path beside it led to two outdoor showers. A tall woman with long shining black hair was riding a horse in the shallow surf. The animal's mane shone like its rider's. Zack asked Marissa to find a set of loungers for them while he grabbed some drinks. When he asked her what she wanted, she asked for a piña colada. He boisterously declared that he wanted a bloody mary. She was walking lazily through the rows of loungers when she heard them.

"Marissa!?" Tom's familiar voice rang out.

He was sitting between David and Cherry.

CHAPTER SIXTEEN

"You're not following us, are you?" Tom said, grinning and lowering his sunglasses.

"Just a coincidence," Marissa replied softly.

"Well, come on. Join us!" David said.

Cherry's Ray-Bans concealed her closed eyes. She was under a thin blanket, sleeping off a hangover. From the corner of her eye, Marissa saw Zack beeline toward her, two drinks in hand.

"Found a spot?" he asked.

"Hey! You must be the boyfriend," David said to Zack.

"Sorry?" Zack said.

"I'm David. This is Tom. And Sleeping Beauty over there's Cherry. We saw you two in Folegandros."

"Oh! You were the guys at the beach, uhh, when it started to rain. I didn't recognize you with clothes on. I'm Zack. This is my girlfriend, Marissa," Zack said.

"Yeah. We've met," Tom said.

"Right," Zack said, remembering seeing them have a brief conversation on the sand while he swam.

They made themselves comfortable on the two loungers next to David. Marissa sipped her piña colada.

"So. Zack. Are you from San Diego too?" David asked.

"Uhh, No. Greenwich, Connecticut. You?"

"I was raised in Madrid and Tom's from Guadalajara."

"Oh wow. That's cool. And how did you two meet?" Zack took a sip of his bloody mary.

"We were both in London for a semester at this art school and I went to one of Tom's exhibitions," David started.

"And he came up to me and started flirting. Telling me how much he liked my work," Tom chimed in.

"So you're both artists?" Zack asked.

"We try," David said. "What about you? How'd you two meet?"

"Oh. It's sort of a cute story. I was at this cocktail bar after work, drinking with some clients and Marissa was a bartender there. I got pretty hammered and went back the next day to see if I could get her number. The rest is history."

"That's adorable," Tom said, sitting up to join the conversation.

"Thanks," Zack replied.

"Why didn't you join us in Folegandros?" David asked.

"Sorry?" Zack looked up with a confused smile.

"When we hung out with Marissa that night. Why didn't you join us?"

Tom elbowed David gently.

"What night?" said Zack.

Marissa's face got red and she turned to Zack to explain.

"The first night there. You got drunk and after I took you back to the hotel I went out for a walk because I couldn't sleep and I ran into these guys having some beers. They invited me to join them and we shared a couple of drinks and chatted for a bit," she said.

"Huh. Why didn't you mention it?" Zack said.

129

David pursed his lips and turned his head to Tom.

"It really wasn't a big deal," Marissa lied. "Wanna walk down the beach?"

"Uhh... I think I'm good. This sunburn's fucking killing me. I'm gonna stay here in the shade. But you should go if you want. I'll just be here," Zack said.

Cherry was snoring softly as Marissa hastily finished her piña colada and started along the beach. The sand was warm and black beneath her. White cliffs confronted the sea, their sheer faces pressing the reach into a narrow, blinding stillness. A cool swash of seafoam brushed Marissa's bare feet as she walked in the wet sand, sobering her with each caress. The horse and its rider, appearing tiny at the far end of the strand, were growing larger in the distance after having turned around at the end of the expanse to begin their return gallop. A lone pelican sat in the calm backline, beyond the gentle surf. It had a vacant yet wise expression, as if it had arrived early to meet an unfortunate fish.

With the sound of the lapping surf, the kiss of the sun on her neck and the perfect amount of alcohol in her system, Marissa felt oddly at ease as she walked, alternating between the warm dry sand and the cool foreshore. She knew Cherry wouldn't betray her confidence and the new introductions actually worked to relax some of the tension she had. The beach was mostly empty until she continued further to the most isolated part. Naked older couples, all with matching leathered skin, sat scattered on towels laid on the dark sand. Half of them were asleep. She took this as a sign to turn back. Having walked half the distance back to the loungers, she saw Cherry coming in her direction. She was wearing a white bikini with pink trim. This time, no earrings.

"Marissa!" She said, greeting her with a hug.

"Hey. How's it going?"

"Not too bad. The guys told me you were here. And with the boyfriend this time?"

"Yeah. Weird coincidence running into each other again. It's a small island."

"Sure. Sure. How're you liking Santorini?"

"The towns were a bit touristy but we just had a pretty nice lunch. What about you? You liking it so far?"

"Yeah. It's nice. Bit different from Folegandros. Bit more energy. Listen. We're going to hit this club later tonight - Enigma. Why don't the two of you join us?"

"I don't know. I don't think Zack's into that kind of thing. And I think he made some dinner reservations."

"No worries. I see you found my Instagram, so just let me know if you change your mind. These things go late."

"Thanks. Hey. Umm... With Zack..."

"Tom and David don't know a thing."

Marissa sighed. The woman on the horse trotted past them. Getting a closer view, they both turned to her and saw the length of her tan legs, her lean torso and her daisy yellow bikini.

"Bit of a lush, isn't she?" Cherry said as she passed.

"Yeah," Marissa agreed.

Together, they walked back to the beachside bar, enjoying the rhythm of the softly lapping waves. When they returned to the shaded loungers, Marissa saw that Tom and David had followed Zack's lead and each ordered a bloody mary. She reclined in the seat next to Zack.

"What're you guys chatting about?" asked Cherry, sitting upright on the edge of her chair.

"Zack was just telling us his uncle's friends with Tommy Hilfiger," David said.

"No shit?" Cherry suppressed a laugh.

"They used to be neighbors," Zack said.

"Before that we were talking about music," said Tom.

"Yeah. We actually have pretty similar taste. Charli XCX, Kelela, DJ Lag..." Zack listed.

"I've heard of Charli, but not the other two," said Cherry, reaching to steal a sip of Tom's bloody mary.

"You know Sinjin Hawke?" Zack asked her.

"Never heard of him," she replied.

"He's great. I saw him at Sonar with Zora Jones a few years back," said David.

"Oh yeah? Where?" Zack had sobered slightly.

"Barcelona."

"Back when you were a club rat," Tom laughed.

"God. That feels like it was ages ago." David leaned his head back.

"That's so fucking cool," Zack said.

"We're going with a group of friends to Enigma tonight if you want to join us," Tom offered. "We don't usually do the whole nightlife thing anymore but we've been coerced."

"Sounds fun. But we have plans later. Maybe we can all link up another time though. You guys on Instagram?" Zack pulled his phone from his pocket.

They exchanged account information. The sun was dipping

lower on the horizon and a soft breeze rolled in from the south. A squadron of pelicans flew parallel to the shore in an arrow.

"I think we're gonna head back to our hotel for a quick nap before dinner," Zack said, addressing the group. "Great to meet you though."

"Same," said Tom.

"Yeah. See you around," David added.

After all the goodbyes, Zack and Marissa walked back up the hill to the dirt lot behind the restaurant and climbed back into the Polaris. They drove a different route back to the hotel, opting for a smaller road that ran through the center of the island. The engine roared too loudly for conversation.

Under an hour later, they arrived at the hotel and walked down the long white staircase to their room. Zack threw off his clothes and grabbed a fresh bottle of water from the coffee table.

"Wanna fuck?" Zack asked.

"Well when you phrase it so eloquently..."

"Darling. Shall we make love?" he said, deepening his voice.

Marissa sighed.

"Yeah. Okay," she said. "Let me take a quick shower first."

"After," he suggested, setting the water bottle on the nightstand.

"I feel gross."

"Then let's have gross sex. I haven't showered either."

"You want me to get an infection?"

"Fine. I'll wait," Zack said before hurling himself on the bed and grabbing his phone.

Marissa stepped into the bathroom and closed the door behind her. She ran the shower and sat on the toilet. While she waited for the water to warm, she scrolled through Cherry's Instagram page, studying her old posts. The mirror was starting to fog, so Marissa disrobed and stepped under the hot water. She took her time, relaxing as she felt the steam on her skin. Twenty minutes later, she turned off the water, towelled dry, and stepped back into the room wearing a bathrobe. Zack was asleep with his hand on his crotch. His phone rested in the open palm of his other hand. There was a video still playing on the screen. A doe eyed woman with brunette bangs was performing fellatio on her astonishingly well endowed partner. Marissa watched the video for a few seconds, then decided to ignore it and let it play. Feeling awake and energized by the shower, she rummaged through her backpack for her last somewhat clean set of clothes. All she had that was unworn was a navy blue crop top and a long white cotton skirt. She also picked out her slightly soiled hoodie and got dressed before grabbing the second novel she'd packed - *Giovanni's Room* by James Baldwin. She was dying for a cigarette, so she opened a new pack of Marlboro Golds and immediately lit one as she stepped out of the room.

She made her way up the stairs to the hotel bar and sat at an outdoor corner table. Catamarans and small yachts littered the surface of the wide channel separating the caldera from the island. Across the room sat a couple. The man had tan muscular arms and wore a tight-fitting blue cotton shirt with khaki pants and brown shoes. He had a very full and well maintained beard of thick black hair. Both his sunglasses and wristwatch reflected sunlight noticeably. The woman across from him had glistening black hair, tied back tightly in a ponytail. Her skin was less tan than his and her breasts filled out an expensive looking white dress. She was adorned with gold and as she grabbed the espresso martini in front of her, her wrist moved very carefully, as if she was picking up a butterfly from a leaf without harming it. The bearded man had a glass of champagne. They were speaking Turkish, but Marissa couldn't understand a word of it. She opened her book, smoked her Gold, and waited to order.

When the waiter came, Marissa asked for a caipirinha then lit another cigarette. Her right eye twitched slightly and she put her index finger up to the soft edge of her inferior lid to feel it and cool her face. Her cocktail arrived moments later. She read a chapter and a half of her book while savoring the flavor. She could taste that it was made with Leblon, just as she had served it to her customers in Manhattan. She was focused on her book when a voice interrupted her.

"Pardon me. I hope I'm not intruding. If you're staying a while, would you care to join me for a drink at the bar?" she heard a man say in a calm baritone. He was tall and hid his eyes behind sunglasses. He had a neatly trimmed beard with dark hair that was starting to whiten in spots and wore a gray suit. Putting her book down and looking up at him, Marissa estimated his age to be somewhere in the late fifties.

"I'm sorry. I'm actually here with my boyfriend," she said.

"I'm here with my wife. My invitation is completely innocent. A drink is always more enjoyable when it's shared, but please, feel free to continue reading. Again, sorry to bother you."

"Well... I'd be happy to join you but I don't think they'll let me smoke at the bar," she put her bookmark on the page.

"Of course you may smoke. Your name?" he asked.

"Marissa," she said, standing up.

"Oskar. Nice to meet you," he led her to the bar and pulled out a leather backed stool for her. "And what will you be having, Marissa?"

"I'm not sure. I just had a caipirinha. Maybe something similar?"

Oskar waved at the bartender and ordered two corpse revivers.

"Number two," he specified. "Have you ever tried this?"

"I have, yeah. I was a bartender for almost a year," Marissa said.

"That's excellent. For me, mixology is just a hobby. Where did you work?"

"A place called Little Branch in New York."

"Beautiful city. You're from there?"

"Well, I live there now but I was raised in California."

"Ahh. Where in California? If you don't mind my asking."

He took a lacquered S.T. Dupont lighter from his pocket, his movements unhurried, and lit her cigarette before selecting a cigar from a leather case, clipping it, and lighting it. The bartender put a crystal ashtray between them.

"San Diego," she said.

"My daughter lives in Del Mar. She's about your age."

"Oh yeah? How old is that?"

"If I had to guess, I'd say you're somewhere in your early twenties."

"Good guess. Where are *you* from?"

"I've spent the last twenty years in Zurich but I'm originally from Lucerne."

"That's near the mountains, right?"

"Yes. Your geography is good," he smiled.

The bartender placed their cocktails on coasters and set a small bowl of seasoned cashews between them.

"So what brought your daughter to Del Mar?" Marissa asked

before taking a sip.

"She's doing a PhD program at UCSD for cognitive and neurological science."

"Wow." Marissa said, responding both to Oskar and the drink.

Oskar laughed.

"Yes. We're both very proud of her, my wife and I."

"Do you have any other children?"

"Two sons. Both in university. One at Sorbonne and the other at ETH in Zurich."

"I would have loved to study at Sorbonne. I visited Paris once back in college."

"It's never too late. You have youth. There's no reason you couldn't study there if it's what you want to do," he took a sip from his cocktail and puffed on his cigar.

"Well, I don't know. I live with my boyfriend in New York and I have a pretty solid business going for me. We were just talking earlier today about getting a bigger apartment together."

"What is your line of work now?"

"I walk dogs."

"May I offer advice?"

"Sure," Marissa leaned forward.

"I've had a career in finance since I was around your age. I've been married three times. I'm getting old now and I have some regrets in life, just like everybody else. But one thing I don't regret is pushing myself forward. My family wasn't wealthy and I worked hard to educate myself. If you really want to go to Sorbonne, you absolutely should. It will open doors for you that you couldn't imagine. I loved my first wife, but she couldn't tolerate my work hours. Our marriage lasted a little more than a year. I met my second wife a few years later. Things were good for a while. But I was still young and I started earning more money. I took a mistress and my wife started sleeping with our neighbor. She became pregnant by him and we divorced. I'm sorry. I didn't mean to tell you my life story but I've learned from age and experience and raised a wonderful family," Oskar took another sip of his drink. "What I'm trying to say is that you're young. You've got a lot of life ahead of you. The greatest error a person could make is to sacrifice their ambition. And again, I'm sorry if I've spoken out of turn."

"No. I appreciate it. I mean... I get it. Life's short but..."

"Every day is shorter than the one before it."

"But I wouldn't even know how I'd begin something like that. I don't even speak French," Marissa took a long sip of her drink.

"That can be remedied faster than you think. French is an easy language to learn," he finished his corpse reviver, then ordered a whiskey sour.

Marissa declined a second drink. She took out another cigarette and he lit it for her. Oskar looked over Marissa's shoulder to his wife who was walking toward them. She wore a long black cocktail dress. Her natural blond hair fell straight down to her shoulders. She had on a gold Cartier watch and her hips swayed as she walked in heels. She didn't look a day over forty five.

"I see you've made a friend," she said, approaching the two at the bar.

"Anna, this is Marissa. Marissa, my wife Anna."

"Nice to meet you," Anna said, nodding.

"Likewise," Marissa smiled.

"Marissa here is from San Diego." Oskar said to his wife.

"Oh, is that so? What part?" she asked.

"Pacific Beach," Marissa said.

"We've spent some time in La Jolla and Del Mar, but haven't explored that area so much. Is it nice?" Anna asked.

"I wouldn't recommend it," she said. "Thanks again for the drink. It was nice talking to you."

"It was a pleasure. Enjoy the rest of your time here," Oskar said.

"You too," she smiled at the couple then grabbed her book from the counter.

The sun was beginning its descent as Marissa stepped down the long white staircase back to the room. When she opened the French door, Zack woke up.

CHAPTER SEVENTEEN

Generous golden light filtered into the room as Marissa slid open the curtains. Zack sat up and stretched. He checked his watch on the nightstand and swung his legs out of bed, stepping into his boxers.

"Damn. I was out," he said.

"Good nap?"

"Yeah. I needed it. Where'd you go?"

"Just up to the bar. I read a little, had a cocktail..."

"Nice. Was it good?"

"Yeah. I had a caipirinha."

"No. The book," he rubbed his eyes then grabbed a bottle of water from the mini-fridge.

"The first chapter is a little slow but I'm sure it will get better."

"Mmm..."

"What time is our dinner?" Marissa asked, setting her book on the coffee table.

"We have, like, two hours. It's just outside Oia, so we could drive there and walk from the lot,"

"I think I'm going to take a shower."

"You should wait. Let's watch the sunset from the hot tub."

"I don't know. I sort of just wanna shower. It was too hot last night."

"I turned it down a little. You'll be fine."

Zack grabbed his swim trunks from his backpack and changed into them. With mild reluctance, Marissa followed suit, neatly folding her last remaining set of clean clothes after tying on her brown bikini. While she changed and used the restroom, Zack called the front desk and ordered a bottle of Ruinart Blanc de Blancs.

They eased into the hot tub and found the temperature more agreeable than the day before. The golden sky had turned luminescent ochre, striated with amaranth and faintly splashed with crimson. There wasn't a cloud in sight. The sea's surface reflected white.

"So. What do you think of Santorini?" Zack asked, stretching his arms on the side of the tub.

"It's lovely. But I think my favorite island so far has been either Milos or Folegandros,"

"Yeah. Milos was amazing. A perfect first stop really. I miss that little beach we had all to ourselves. We're here just one more night, then it's Syros next before heading back to Athens. It's crazy how fast the time flies."

"I actually thought Athens was amazing. Maybe even better than the islands."

"You're a city girl. I'm an island boy,"

"You're an island boy?" Marissa smiled.

The young hostess who had first greeted them came down the stairs to their patio and set a silver standing bucket full of ice beside the tub. Her other hand held the bottle of champagne and two flutes.

"Good evening Mr. Wilson. I take it you're enjoying your stay?"

"Everything's been lovely. Thank you so much," said Zack.

"Would you like me to open the champagne?" she asked.

"That would be great. Thank you," he replied.

Marissa, already ideally inebriated, was hesitant to drink more, but she didn't say anything. This was their last night in Santorini, and Zack had clearly gone out of his way to make the evening special. He thanked the hostess after she poured two glasses and set the bottle in ice. As she disappeared up the stairs, Zack toasted to their future and took a sip of his champagne. Marissa had a dainty sip and set her glass on the tub's tiled edge. She settled deeper into the warm water, letting her neck receive the heat's full embrace. Zack excused himself to grab his phone and returned in less than a minute. He eased back into the water, then set his champagne glass on the tile so he could take a picture of it, the sunset in the background. Once he captured a decent one, he immediately posted it to his Instagram story.

"Babe. Come here," he said to Marissa, setting his phone down.

She came up next to him. They sat side by side, watching the color change as the sun touched the rim of the caldera. He wrapped his arm around her shoulder then started speaking in a calm low voice.

"You know? This is everything for me. This is why I work so hard. Not just being here, but being here with you. Like, look at this moment. We're in a hot tub in Santorini watching a sunset, drinking champagne. We're going out to dinner soon at the best restaurant on the island. It's insane. I mean, People come here for their honeymoons. It's such a blessing that we can even be here and do this. And I'm so happy to be able to share it with you."

"Zack. That's so sweet."

"I'm serious. I couldn't imagine being here with anybody else. I love you Marissa."

"I love you too."

They shared a long kiss. The thinning sky took on a periwinkle shade and the roof of the heavens was darkening slowly, inviting stars to dance, one by one.

"You know, I saw something weird earlier. Down the cliff from us. I wanna show you," Zack said.

"What is it?"

"You just have to come see."

"I really have to get up right now? Out of the water?"

"Just for a few seconds. I'll get your bathrobe."

"Okay. But just for a few seconds."

Zack went inside and came out with her robe. Marissa stepped out of the tub.

"Okay. What is it?" she asked.

They walked to the edge of their patio, where there were no rooms beneath them. From there was a steep dry hillside with a few scattered trees. In the sea below, half a dozen catamarans were anchored, their chefs grilling meat while guests watched the sunset.

"Look out there," Zack said, pointing at the horizon.

"What are you pointing at?"

"You don't see it?"

"I don't know what you want me to see."

"Just wait."

Marissa looked directly at the horizon where Zack was pointing. There was nothing unusual, just the sanguine line softly tinted green where the sky met the sea. The sun disappeared behind the caldera and the lights on the boats came on, shining on a darkened surface like stars in the night.

"Just tell me what you wan..." she turned around to Zack.

He was down on his left knee, his right leg at a sharp ninety degree angle. In his left hand was a small red box with gold trim.

"I've known from the moment I saw you that I wanted to spend the rest of my life with you. You're the most amazing person I've ever met and you're my best friend. I love your smile and your laugh and your eyes, and everything else that makes you who you are. So I'm asking you, Marissa Rose Neuman, will you marry me?"

He opened the box and inside shone a two carat marquise cut diamond set into a simple platinum band. Even in the fading light, the stone radiated prismatic fire, refracting every color of every sunset.

Marissa held her hands over her mouth and looked down into Zack's eyes. He looked up at her like one of the begging cats.

"Oh. Zack," she said softly.

He took a deep breath. She turned her head and shivered. Tears welled up in her eyes. She wanted to speak, but words struggled to leave her mouth and she couldn't think of exactly what she needed to say.

"Zack," she repeated.

"Yes?" he said.

"I'm sorry. I can't do this."

"Marissa, I..."

"Stand up Zack."

"I know it's sudden and we haven't talked about it, but I'm so serious."

"Yeah. I know you are. And..."

"Do you love me?" he asked, his eyes watering.

"Of course I do, but like, that's not enough to get married. I'm only twenty four."

"It doesn't mean we have to get married immediately."

"I just don't know Zack. I don't know."

"Well I know."

"How? I mean, like, how could you be so sure? We're young. And like, all we've done this trip is argue and get drunk."

"That's not all we did."

"It really is. How do you even know that you love me? How do you know that you don't just love love?"

"I love you so much Marissa. You mean everything to me. Just please say yes."

"I can't."

Zack's expression soured and the night turned dark. He closed the box and stood up.

"Fuck. I mean..." he laughed aggressively. "What the fuck? Like... Yeah, I know we didn't discuss this but I really thought you'd say yes. We've been together long enough for me to know I want to spend my life with you but you clearly don't feel the same way. I guess I should have waited more before asking."

Marissa sighed and wiped away a tear.

"I just think you're the coolest person I've ever met," he said, starting to cry.

"Come on Zack. Please don't cry," she took his arm and they walked over to the table. He set the box on it and they both sat down.

"I'll be fine. I'm sorry. Forget I asked. Let's just go to dinner. Let's just try to have a good time tonight."

"I don't know..."

"What do you mean you don't know?"

"Like, what are we doing? Is this really a healthy relationship?

145

Sometimes I feel like you treat me like more of an object than a person."

"What the fuck are you talking about? I've always been respectful and kind,"

"Then why do we argue, like, every day?"

"You tell me."

"I just... I feel like I may have been falling out of love with you."

"Wow. Okay."

Marissa composed herself. She sat upright and tightened her expression, showing no hint of emotion.

"I'm sorry Zack, but that's just how I've been feeling. Can you really say you haven't felt it too?"

"I love you completely. I don't want to lose you," he sighed. "I'm sorry I rushed things. Let's take our time and maybe take it slower from now on."

"You're not hearing me. I don't think I can do this anymore."

"I don't understand."

"I know you don't, but things add up."

"Just please give me another chance," he was crying. "Let's just forget about this. Let me take you to dinner."

"I cheated on you."

His tears stopped and he suddenly felt the cold wind on his wet shoulders. Goosebumps overwhelmed him and although he was cold, he didn't shiver.

"When?" he asked, his voice moving down a register.

"In Folegandros."

"Are you fucking serious?"

"The night you got drunk. I went out drinking and I met

somebody and we hooked up."

"Wow. Okay," Zack stood up.

Marissa sighed and looked at the caldera's silhouette.

"Fuck..." he said, almost laughing. "Here I am thinking you're the one. And you're just another fucking slut. I should have known better."

"Yeah. Okay. Here it comes," she said, crossing her arms.

"You unappreciative whore. Do you know how much I paid for this trip? Do you have any idea how much this ring cost?"

Marissa laughed.

"You fucking cheat on me, during a vacation that I worked hard for and then you fucking laugh?"

"What the fuck do you want from me, Zack? What? You want me to fuck you every day and be a perfect wife but it's not like you ever consider what I want. I didn't even want to come here. You disrespect me constantly..."

"How? What's one time I've disrespected you?"

"You literally fell asleep watching porn this afternoon. You drink way too much. You..."

"I never cheated on you."

Marissa went silent.

"Sure. I watch porn sometimes. Who cares? You fucking cheated on me. You had another guy's dick inside you."

"That's not true."

"No? Well than what the fuck are you talking about? What happened?"

"It was a woman."

"That blonde from the beach?"

147

Marissa sighed.

"Wow," Zack laughed. "You could have just brought her back to our room."

"She's not into guys."

"Well clearly neither are you," he grabbed the red box from the table. "You know what? Fuck you and fuck this. When we get back to New York, I want you and your shit gone."

"Fine."

Zack grabbed the champagne bottle and took a swig, then he went inside and changed into dry clothes, packing his wet swimsuit directly in his backpack. Marissa followed him in while he hurriedly packed his things.

"You know, I thought we could've spent the rest of our lives together. I fucking loved you Marissa."

"That doesn't matter anymore. I'm sorry Zack."

"Yeah. Whatever." he wiped a tear.

He had his backpack slung over his shoulder as he stood in front of the open French door. She was still wearing her bathrobe. He turned to look at her, taking in her green eyes, her wavy brunette hair, trying to remember what her skin felt like in his hands.

"Want to have sex one last time before I go?" he asked.

She shook her head.

"I'm sorry," she said coldly.

"No. You're not."

CHAPTER EIGHTEEN

When the bus parked in the dirt lot at Fira, Marissa was the first to step out. A cold wind pierced her denim jacket and ruffled her skirt. The last days of an extended summer had ended and November was just around the corner. She followed the map on her phone through the town, passing laughing groups of friends and couples eating ice cream. Music from previous decades played loudly in restaurant speakers and soft light touched the flagstone path, yellowing its veins.

There was a small queue in front of the club, and Marissa took her place in it. Stepping through the warm doorway, she took some relief from the cold, but found herself almost immediately missing the chilled wind. *No Broke Boys* by Disco Lines and Tinashe was blasting on the sound system and a convivial yet acrid air permeated the low ceilinged room. Purple lights colored the walls and the dance floor was already packed and dark. A red and white strobe flickered, allowing Marissa to spot Cherry's achromatic hair. It seemed whiter in the unnatural glow. She had positioned herself by the wall, bouncing to the rhythm with a drink in her hand, her cherry earrings swaying as her body moved. Most of the gang surrounded her.

"Hey. Mind if I join you?" Marissa asked loudly but still unheard over the song.

"Marissa!" Danny shouted, turning to hug her.

The guys all turned to her and smiled, except for Tom and David, already drunk and attached to each other. Cherry had her eyes closed and was locked in a trance.

"Do you have a drink?" he yelled into Marissa's ear.

"What?" she couldn't hear him.

"Drink?" he repeated, leaning in more.

"Oh. Sure," she replied.

She followed him to a crowded bar where a squad of young bartenders all wearing tight black shirts looked dead inside. They were serving only vodka tonics. Danny paid for her and got another for himself. When she sipped it, it tasted more like tonic than alcohol. The song changed to Hudson Mohawke's remix of *Mannequin Love* by Justice.

Cherry noticed Marissa when she returned to the group, drink in hand. She unleashed a wide smile and hugged her. She was sweaty but Marissa couldn't tell if it was her own or a foul blend of every clubgoer's liquids stuck to her flesh.

"You made it!" Cherry yelled.

Marissa smiled and nodded, then took a sip of her tonic. Cherry grabbed her free arm and they danced. The music was far too loud for conversation, even in moments of decrescendo.

"Great DJ!" Isaac yelled at them.

The purple and red lights along with the thumping bass enraptured Marissa and, in that moment, she felt free. The track transitioned to *Are You In?* by DJ Seinfeld and by now, the whole dancefloor was under hypnosis. Somebody approached the group and handed out sparklers. Marissa closed her eyes as she bounced and at the exact moment she finished her watered down drink, Charlie came with a fresh round and they all toasted and continued the festivity. The DJ switched the track to *Bye Vibes* by Samantha Barrón and Cherry put her hand on Marissa's hip. Their movements grew more and more sensual as the song progressed. Next up was *Calabria 2008* by Enur.

Marissa didn't know how long she'd been there, but her afternoon of continuous drinking paired with the deceivingly strong vodka tonics warped her perception of time. When the song switched to *Gimme! Gimme! Gimme!*, Marissa pulled a cigarette from her pocket and made eye contact with Cherry. She nodded in understanding and the two stepped outside to smoke.

"Glad you made it!" Cherry said, lighting a Touch Blue.

"Me too," Marissa said, taking the lighter from her.

"Where's the boyfriend?"

"Lord knows. I'm just trying to have a good time."

"Had a fight?"

"Big one."

Their body's heat broke the wind.

"Well, you're here now. Let's do exactly that," Cherry said.

"That's the plan. How long have you guys been here?"

"Not too long. Maybe an hour before you showed up."

"Nice. I'm trying to get fucked up tonight."

"You're not already?" Cherry laughed.

"I guess I might be. But I mean, I wanna get absolutely faded."

"Must have been a big argument."

"I don't even want to think about it."

"Sorry I brought it up."

"Don't worry about it. You ready to head back in?" Marissa

tossed her cigarette.

"Let's go," Cherry said, doing the same.

The buildup of *Honey* by Caribou was playing as they made their way through the crowd back to their spot. Rob handed them a new drink and Marissa chugged hers and tossed the plastic cup on the floor. She closed her eyes and let the music take her. The purple light grew dimmer. The next song was Slayyyter's *No Comma* and half way through, Marcus tapped Marissa's shoulder and made eye contact.

"Your turn," he shouted.

"What?" she yelled back.

"Next round. Your turn!" he said, holding up his empty cup.

Marissa nodded then made her way to the bar. The bartender asked her how many and she told him nine. He pressed some numbers into a card reader and slid it to her. One hundred and forty four euros.

Sixteen euros per drink. She had no choice so she inserted her card in the reader and saw the charge go through. It occurred to her, at that moment, that during the previous two weeks, she'd spent very little money and this was the second largest charge of the trip - the other being the restaurant in Folegandros where Zack had ordered a whole sea bream. The bartender quickly filled nine plastic cups and set them on a circular tray, which Marissa very carefully brought to the group. *Treat Each Other Right* by Jamie xx was playing now, then came on Only Fire's remix of *5G* by Heidi Montag. Marissa made her next drink last a little longer after realizing how expensive it was.

She was drunk and dehydrated when Marcus handed her another cup and Cobrah's *Brand New Bitch* was playing. She was starting to get a headache, so she set her drink down and went outside for another cigarette. In the cold air outside the club, she pulled her pack from her breast pocket and saw it was empty. She closed her eyes and sighed.

"Need a light?" she heard Cherry say.

"I need a smoke," she gestured at the empty box.

Cherry handed her a Touch Blue and lit it for her. It tasted soft and familiar.

"I think I'm drunk. I'm getting a headache," Marissa said.

"Should we get out of here? I actually hate this electronic shit. It's not my vibe at all but the boys love it."

"I'm down. Where to?"

"Well, I'm guessing your place is out of the question, so we can walk from here to my Airbnb if you're up for it."

"Sure. I'd like that," Marissa took a long drag.

"You hungry?" Cherry asked.

"Not really,"

"I'm fucking starving. I think I'll grab something on the way back."

"Maybe I should eat too, to soak up the alcohol."

"Great. I'm just gonna head inside and say a quick goodbye to the guys."

"Cool. Take your time," she said, enjoying her cigarette slowly.

Cherry went inside. Marissa finished her Touch Blue and tossed the butt into the street, not bothering to extinguish it. She waited two minutes in the cold with nothing to smoke before Cherry emerged. They staggered drunkenly through the dimly lit flagstone paths until they got to the main road. Marissa sat in a plastic chair outside a gyro stand while Cherry ordered two of them. She came back with two bottles of water and offered Marissa another cigarette, which she accepted like a bird taking bread.

"So. What's next after this?" Cherry asked.

"What?" Marissa replied.

"I mean which island are you off to next?"

Marissa thought for fifteen seconds. She still had her ferry tickets on her phone, but she wasn't sure what she should do. She hadn't given it any thought.

"I don't know," she said.

"You're just gonna play it by ear?"

"Well we were supposed to go to... Syros, I think. But we just broke up so I don't even know anymore."

"You broke up in Santorini!?" Cherry twisted open her water bottle.

"He proposed to me earlier."

"Ahhh. I see."

"I know, right!?"

"And it was out of the blue?"

"We'd never talked about it."

"What an idiot."

"No. He was sweet actually. I'm an idiot."

"We're young. Fuck that kind of life. Who wants to be married in their twenties and have kids before they're thirty? I can't imagine being a fifty year old grandmother. I mean, fuck having kids altogether. Sounds like an absolute nightmare."

"Well it doesn't matter now. I don't even have a place to go home to."

"Maybe you can work things out."

"I don't know."

"Hold that thought," Cherry said, getting up to grab the gyros.

Marissa nibbled at hers slowly while Cherry downed hers with gusto. Marissa felt her head spinning and tried to fight the urge to vomit by closing her eyes and resting her head in her hands. The effort only made it worse and she excused herself to the restroom and made a mess of the toilet. *Probably not the first time this has happened here,* she thought as she cleaned herself in the sink.

"You alright?" Cherry asked, watching her walk slowly back to the table.

"Yeah. Fine. Should we head out?"

"Let's do it."

They walked next to each other as dark clouds rolled in. Small droplets of rain appeared on Cherry's shoulders, shining like black diamonds on the leather. They got to Cherry's room in a few minutes. It was small, with a single window looking out on a narrow alley. A double bed occupied most of the room and behind it was a door to an unaccommodating restroom. Cherry switched on the lights and threw her jacket on the floor. Marissa excused herself to brush her teeth with her finger and when she had finished, Cherry was lying on the bed wearing only a tank top and panties. Her earrings sat on the nightstand next to her pack of Touch Blues. Marissa pulled down her long white skirt and tossed it on the floor along with her denim jacket and lay down next to Cherry.

They kissed as rain pattered harder on the window. Cherry grabbed Marissa's breast then caressed her side and continued down to her thigh. She slowly removed Marissa's panties and started using her tongue. Marissa closed her eyes and her breath quickened. After a few minutes, Cherry started using her finger. First one, then two. Marissa moaned then pulled off her crop top and unhooked her bra. Cherry followed suit and after Marissa climaxed, she did her best to reciprocate the pleasure. It felt natural - unforced. After they'd both had an orgasm, they lay naked under the blankets and shared a cigarette.

"You know, you're the first woman I've been with," said Marissa.

"It doesn't seem like it."

"Yeah?"

"Yeah. You certainly know what you're doing." Cherry exhaled the pale blue smoke and handed the cigarette to Marissa. "You given any more thought as to what's next?"

"I don't know. When I go back to New York, I probably have to find a new place. Fuck. I wish I could just keep traveling forever like you."

"I mean, eventually I'll have to figure my shit out, I guess. Money doesn't last forever. But maybe I'll find a place and a gig and I can put down some roots for a while."

"Do you think you'll ever go back to Perth?"

"No. Not any time soon. I'm flying to Rome in a few days. Gonna crash on my friend's couch. After that, who knows?"

"That should be fun. But, like, don't you think it may be a good idea to visit home? Just for a little while?"

"Why?" Cherry sat up and grabbed another cigarette.

"I don't know. Isn't it, like, better to confront trauma head on?"

"Are you serious? I barely know you Marissa. Who the fuck are you to tell me what to do?"

"Sorry. I didn't mean it like that,"

"Like, what the fuck? You don't hear me asking you shit like this. Why don't you worry about your own family and your fucked up relationship?"

"I'm sorry!"

"I opened up to you because I like you," Cherry lit her cigarette.

"I like you too. I'm sorry."

The rain was pouring now and streaks of water ran down the window.

"I think maybe you should go," Cherry said.

"Please let me stay here. I don't want to be alone."

"Marissa. What do you think this is?"

"I don't know," she said, her eyes starting to water.

"This was a fling. On vacation. It's not like we're a couple."

"I mean, I..."

"I'm not trying to hurt your feelings Marissa. I had fun. We both did. But you have a life to get back to. I don't. Why don't you go make it work with your boyfriend. I'm sure he'll be happy to get back together."

"Now *you're* telling me what I should do?" Marissa reached over to grab another cigarette.

"Doesn't feel so good when the shoe's on the other foot, does it?"

"Look. I'm sorry. It's raining. Can't I just stay the night?"

"I had fun. But I think I'd rather be alone tonight. There are cabs down on the main street."

"You're serious?"

Cherry got out of bed and walked to the bathroom, then closed the door. Marissa got up and followed her.

157

"You're going to make me go back to the hotel to spend the night with my ex?" she said through the closed door.

"Nobody's making you do anything Marissa. I don't get why you're being so difficult."

"I just thought, maybe, we could have been something more."

Cherry opened the door. The two stood naked under the overhead light, facing each other.

"What on earth made you think that? How would you expect that to work? We've spent no more than a few hours together. You're fucking delusional."

"I really like you."

"Yes Marissa. I like you too. This was fun. But be serious. This was a fling. Do I have to spell it out for you? We're not a couple. We smoke. We drink. We fuck. That's it. I don't get why you can't be mature about this."

"So you just fucking used me?"

Cherry laughed.

"How on earth did I use you?" she said.

"I don't know. I guess that's just what you do. You travel around and sleep with people to make yourself feel better."

"My God, Marissa. That's what people do. If anything, you used me. But I don't care. It's fine. I don't want to argue with you. Just please go," Cherry said calmly. She brushed past Marissa as she grabbed her panties from the floor and put them back on. "Look," she said, sitting on the bed. "I'm sorry. If it means anything, I do feel bad about it. You can stay if you want. But I think I might go out again."

"You know what? Fuck it. I'll go," Marissa rushed to put her clothes back on. "Have a good life Cherry. I hope you find what you're looking for."

"Likewise,"

Marissa stepped out into the rain and sobbed. She felt cold and it took only a few minutes for her skirt to become soaked. She passed a small line of taxis and ignored them. As she walked along the side of the main road, the rain let up slightly and the clouds parted for a brief moment, allowing the moonlight to shine on the calm empty sea.

There was no sign of Zack when Marissa got back to the room. His backpack and all his effects were gone. The unfinished bottle of champagne, now flat, sat beside the table in a bucket of rainwater and melted ice. Marissa heaved a deep sigh before stepping out of her wet clothes then draping them over the coffee table. She turned on the hotel room's heater, then opened a new pack of Marlboro Golds. She lit one in the room then opened the French door to exhale the smoke. She tied her hair into a ponytail then stepped naked onto the balcony and eased into the hot tub, letting the gentle rain massage her face.

CHAPTER NINETEEN

By the next morning, the storm had passed. Marissa sipped a freddo espresso at a café by the port, her backpack resting in the seat next to her. Seagulls lingered on the concrete and families sat beside her at the neighboring tables, eating fried pies and going through photos on their phones. The ferry had just rounded the caldera and was steaming into port as Marissa left a few coins on the table and made her way to the open-air waiting room.

She'd woken up very late. Marissa felt guilty waking up alone for the first time in weeks, stretching in the excessively sized bed. The unchanged sheets still smelled like Zack. She showered and made herself an espresso in the room, which she drank on the couch while listening to the new Taylor Swift album. The relief she felt listening to the album for the first time, undisturbed, worked slightly to help her forget the events of the previous evening but by the end of her coffee, guilt crept back into her. She quickly packed her things and went upstairs to the reception desk to discover that the room and all the additional charges had already been paid for. She thanked the receptionist and walked up to the street. The same van took her down to the port.

She boarded the *Eurochampion Jet* as part of a herd of tourists - many of them heading straight to Mykonos. Her ticket was already paid for and so she figured she should continue the journey instead of booking new accommodation. She found a seat on the deck and lit a cigarette as the ferry casted off. Finding herself truly alone for the first time in weeks, curiosity got the best of her and she decided to check Zack's Instagram page. No new posts. No new stories. He was just gone. She thought about messaging him but couldn't find the words, so she went to Cherry's page. She'd reposted some pictures from the club onto her story and Marissa saw that she appeared in none of them. With her Marlboro Gold half smoked, she pulled *Giovanni's Room* out of her backpack and began devouring the pages. Strong sunlight shone on the calm sea and shore birds trailed the ferry's wake. Three hours later, Marissa had finished her last pack of cigarettes along with two fifths of the novel and arrived in Ermoupoli.

The city was louder than she'd expected - definitely not what she'd experienced on any of the other islands. Palm trees and tapas bars lined the seaside road that wrapped around the harbor. Still feeling hungover, lightheaded, and slightly seasick, she crossed the street to escape the noise of each bar's speaker system playing a different beat and walked along the sidewalk that doubled as a seawall. The boats usually moored there were all out, so Marissa's view of the horizon was unobstructed. The sunlight was intense and she felt it on her cheeks and shoulders. An old man with leathered skin and a faded cap sat on a wooden chair and held a fishing pole to the sea. Under an awning a few steps away, a group of middle aged women sat drinking aperol spritz and loudly speaking Spanish.

Ermoupoli was built on the side of a hill. All the buildings stood tall and gave each other shade. Overlooking the city, at the top of the hill stood a church, domed in turquoise. Marissa decided to shelter from the oppressive sunlight by walking deeper into the city and found a street full of stores. She stopped inside one to buy a new set of underwear and a t-shirt with a starfish on it. She was starting to sweat under her backpack, so she looked up the cheapest hotel she could find and started up the hill in its direction. When she opened a heavy door to enter the lobby, she found it to be a white tiled room, no larger than a freight elevator, with a small black desk in the corner. At the desk sat a young woman with black hair and glasses staring at a laptop. Behind her was a small closet filled with cleaning supplies, its door cracked open. All the walls were white and not a single piece of art adorned any of them. A sad looking split-leaf philodendron in a plastic pot occupied the corner opposite the desk.

"Hello. May I help you?" the woman asked.

"Hi. I just need a room for one night please," Marissa said, grabbing her backpack straps.

"Okay. I need your passport please. How many beds?"

"Whatever's least expensive."

"Okay. That's seventy five euro. Will you be paying with card or cash?"

"Card please. You don't have anything cheaper?"

"Sorry. That's our lowest price room."

"It's fine. I'll take it," she handed the woman her debit card.

"One night?" she asked to confirm.

"Yes please, Efcharistó."

"Parakalo."

The woman handed back the passport and debit card as well as a card key in a blank white envelope with the number 104 written in sharpie. Marissa walked up a narrow staircase beside the reception desk. The hallway reeked of urine. She pressed the card key to the magnetic reader and pushed open the door to her room. It was dark and similarly unadorned, like an extension of the lobby. A single bed with gray sheets stood against an empty white wall and the small bathroom was tiled the same as the lobby. The odor wasn't as foul, but still, she opened the window to let in fresh air. It opened to the street, and a mixed gender group of teenagers were laughing and playfully pushing each other around below. She figured them to be local.

After taking her second shower of the day and changing into her newly purchased underwear, she desperately wanted a cigarette but remembered she'd smoked her last pack on the ferry. She stepped into a dirty pair of jeans and put on her starfish t-shirt then ventured back outside. Remembering having seen a tobacco stand by the port, she retraced her steps. The Spanish speaking women had moved on from their watering hole but the old man remained seated in the same fixed position, statuesque, intently watching the sea. Marissa went into the store and bought two packs of Touch Blues.

She ripped off the plastic wrap and tossed it on the sidewalk then lit a cigarette, inhaling the smoke deeply before tilting her head to the sun. In the harbor, a sixty foot yacht was slowly coming into port. Marissa watched as the crewmen tied it to the mooring on the sidewalk by the old man. The vessel blocked the sun and cast a shadow over him. As the old man reeled in his empty line and slowly packed his things, a lightly tanned man wearing sunglasses, a blue half-buttoned Zegna shirt with white linen shorts, and calfskin Prada loafers stepped across the gangway and said something to one of the crewmen before crossing the street in the direction of a tapas bar.

Marissa tossed her cigarette butt on the sidewalk then decided to walk up the hill to get a better view of the city. As she continued up the steps that ran between the houses, she saw less and less people. A small cat, brown with green eyes, looked up at her then started running away as Marissa approached. Instinctively she followed it. It ran slowly, stopping to look back at her before turning a corner. Marissa followed the cat for about five minutes, running up the steps, zigzagging between narrow streets. As she ran, she didn't notice the bougainvilleas covering the yellow walled houses, or the pigeons perched on railings, watching her. She didn't turn around to notice slivers of the harbor view from the narrow paths higher on the hill. Eventually, the cat stopped in front of a house where two young men with curly black hair sat outside on a ledge, sunbathing in swim trunks and unbuttoned linen shirts. One of them lowered his sunglasses for a moment to look at Marissa, then pushed them back up and closed his eyes again. The cat sat beside them and curled its body before closing its eyes.

Winded, Marissa realized how close she was to the church so she continued up the path and reached the courtyard. A few people sat individually on the ledge. A young woman was reading a book; another was doing something on her phone. An old lady was feeding stale breadcrumbs to a group of pigeons. Marissa turned around to see the town from the top of the hill but the view was obstructed by tall mastic trees, their leaves thick, never surrendering to the seasons. She lit another cigarette then walked around the side of the church to a smaller courtyard where eight old Greek men sat smoking cigarillos and engaging in conversation. From where they rested was the only unobstructed view of the city but Marissa didn't want to disturb them, so she started down the hill.

Weaving aimlessly through the narrow streets, she wondered where Zack had gone. She'd used the ferry ticket he'd purchased and emailed to her but she hadn't seen him on the boat. He hadn't called or texted since their argument at the hotel. She figured that he must have taken a taxi directly to the Santorini airport and purchased a ticket to New York. Marissa's return ticket was from Athens so, as she slowly strolled through the streets and chain smoked her new pack of Touch Blues, she realized she would have to spend the night in Ermoupoli then take the ferry back to Athens and hang out there for a few more days before flying back to New York.

She stopped to light another cigarette and a small gust prevented her lighter from working. She tried igniting it for twenty seconds before getting frustrated and throwing it as well as her cigarette on the ground. She crouched down, cupped her head in her hands and started crying. The same group of teenagers she'd seen earlier walked past her, their laughter unceasing as though Marissa was a ghost. When she noticed their joviality, she wiped her tears and picked up her lighter. She grabbed another cigarette from her pack, then found a windowsill where she could shelter the flame from the breeze. The smoke tasted rancid in her mouth. She continued down the hill to a central plaza where the capitol building stood. Children were running around, scaring flocks of pigeons while their grandmothers watched them. A vendor was selling pies and candies from a colorful stall. While walking through the unshaded plaza, she realized how thirsty she was so she headed back into the shaded alleys and found a tavern. She sat at a table outside and ordered a bottle of water.

"Is that all?" the waiter asked, possibly annoyed that she would take a table just for water.

"I'll have a look at the beverage menu please," she said.

He handed her a full menu from a pocket in his apron, then went inside to grab her a bottle of water. When he returned, she ordered a plate of fried calamari and a Singapore sling. She poured herself a glass of water then lit another cigarette. She looked up to take in the scenery. She was alone outside, eating in between standard meal hours. On her table was white paper, held in place with metal clips and above her, bougainvillea branches woven through a trellis formed a roof. The sun shone through the pink leaves like stained glass. With suspicious haste, the waiter returned with the calamari and the cocktail. The first thing Marissa noticed was a cherry floating with the ice cubes at the rim of the glass.

She picked it out and threw it on the floor.

CHAPTER TWENTY

The city's lights glowed yellow and touched the underbelly of the low clouds. Night had fallen and the boats had all come into port. The bars facing the sea were all full and, from them, laughter and loud music mingled with the cool sea air. Kids were running around the streets unsupervised, laughing and eating gyros. Marissa was lying in bed, trying to focus on *Giovanni's Room*. As she read, her thoughts strayed and she eventually gave up. She played *Summertime Sadness* by Lana Del Rey on her phone's tinny speakers and got up to smoke a cigarette in the windowsill. The song repeated and she tapped out the cigarette on the side of the building before tossing the butt into the street. She thought about lighting another one, but decided to head outside for some fresh air. She put on her shoes, slipped her phone and wallet in her pocket, threw on her jacket, and went down to the street.

She walked in the direction of the port, for no reason other than to hear the lapping of the waves against the seawall. Madonna's *Hung Up* throbbed from the yacht, the unnatural sound muffled and echoing through the air; tall women danced awkwardly in long white dresses on the deck. Marissa picked up her pace as she passed the festivity. She continued along the sea, away from the port until she reached the backside of a grand hotel. Looking through the large glass windows that faced the sea, she saw old couples sitting for dinner and waiters in black vests bringing them wine lists. Marissa sat on the edge of the breakwater and lit a cigarette. As a force of habit, she took her phone from her pocket and opened Instagram. The first thing she noticed was that Zack had posted a story. She hesitated for a moment then decided to open it. It was a picture of him visibly drunk with his friend, Noah, on a boat in an Amsterdam canal. She put her phone back in her pocket. Droplets of water touched her face and she couldn't tell if they were rain or seaspray. The ocean surface was lacquered black and the sound of the waves produced a soothing lull as the low rolling clouds masked the moonlight. The tip of Marissa's cigarette glowed orange as she inhaled, and a pale ribbon of smoke rose from it, spiraling towards the mist before losing its form to the breeze.

The thought of drinking at the bar of the grand hotel entered her mind briefly, but she reasoned that she'd been spending too much and wasn't in the mood to talk to anyone. She continued up the road from the hotel onto a side street with narrow alleys like branches that ran to the dark sea. A few cigarettes later, boredom struck and she made her way back to her room. She took a hot shower then fell asleep.

Marissa woke to the sound of rain falling on the roof across the street from her open window. The sky was matted silver and the downpour fell straight through the stillness. She brushed her teeth, took a moment to check the mirror, then wrapped her body in a blanket and lit a cigarette in the windowsill. Her skin felt cold in the autumnal morning chill and the smoke wafted into her eyes. She forced herself to smoke most of it even though she was thirsty. After tossing the butt into the rain, she threw the blanket onto the bed and filled a glass with tap water. It had an odd taste, slightly brackish and alkaline. Her stomach growled and she realized she had only eaten half a plate of calamari in the last twenty four hours.

After packing her things and putting on the same clothes she wore the day before, she checked out and found a café nestled in an alley near the port. She ordered a freddo espresso and a piece of halvadopita. At a corner table, a group of old men wearing fishermen's caps sat silently drinking Greek coffee. For a moment, Marissa felt out of place, as if her whole day in Ermoupoli had been a dream - but then her coffee arrived. It was the finest pull of espresso she'd ever tasted. Liquid sunshine. And the sweet pie complimented it perfectly. She finished it and ordered a second round.

The windless rain continued steadily. The ferry back to Athens was set to leave in an hour so she paid for her breakfast, left a two euro tip, then stepped out to light a cigarette under an awning. She walked through the rain, holding her Touch Blue vertically so as to not get it wet, and noticed the bars surrounding the port were dead in the morning. Some were open and had handwritten signs advertising breakfast menus but they were all empty. Reaching the end of the road, near the grand hotel, she smelled the aroma of spinning lamb and pork coming from a restaurant. She walked up to the window to investigate and read on the door that they would open at the same time her boat was set to depart.

She returned to the same spot on the breakwater where she'd sat the night before. In the scattered daylight, the droplets of rain fell on a peaceful sea - their ripples expanding and gently colliding with each other. Each time they met, they changed, eventually losing their form and becoming part of the whole.

Her clothes were wet when she crossed the gangplank, boarding the *Blue Star Paros*. She set her backpack on a seat inside, sat down next to it, and immediately started feeling seasick. The cabin was empty so she left her things in her seat and stepped outside onto the deck. The diesel engine roared and the wind made it impossible to light her cigarette. The cold rain softly needled her cheeks. She sighed, tossed her wet unsmoked cigarette in a bin, then looked out at the horizon. Where the sea met the sky was obscured and without edge. A mellow wind blew on the ocean surface, softly chopping the waves and tilting the rain. Marissa leaned against the guardrail and gazed at the matted Aegean, its gray expanse holding her in a gentle embrace.